Love
takes
time

Love
takes
time

ADRIANNE
BYRD

ARABESQUE®

Recycling programs
for this product may
not exist in your area.

SURRENDER

ISBN-13: 978-0-373-83117-3
ISBN-10:   0-373-83117-X

To Eliot
My Rock

Acknowledgments

To my family and friends, thanks for all the support and love that you've given me. To my editor, Evette Porter, thanks for loving my stories. To my wonderful fans and readers, thank you for allowing me to do what I do. It's always a pleasure to entertain you.

I wish you all the best of love,

Adrianne

Prologue

One day Quentin and I will walk down the aisle.

Sighing dreamily, Alyssa twirled around with her arms stretched high above her head. Quentin Dwayne Hinton, her real-life Prince Charming. True, all the Hinton men were handsome, but Quentin had something extra—something special.

Dizzy, she giggled aloud and then bumped into her father. "Oh," she gasped. "Sorry, Dad. I didn't see you."

Alfred Jansen, Roger Hinton's personal chef, was a six-foot-four robust man with a long, silver mane of hair and matching goatee that made him look more like a mountain lion than a man. His commanding presence garnered immediate respect and he certainly ran the Hintons' kitchen with iron authority, but underneath, everyone knew this lion was nothing but a kitten at heart.

"Alyssa, honey. You have to get out of the way. We're trying to get ready for the wedding." Alfred smiled as he reprimanded his daughter. He'd always found it difficult to scold her and everyone knew it.

"I'm sorry, Dad. I'll get out of the way."

The florist and her assistants rushed around the father-and-daughter pair, setting up the arrangements, while one guy ran past with a birdcage of doves.

"Oh, Daddy, look. They're going to release birds."

"Uh-huh." He grabbed her by the hand. "Too bad you're going to miss it."

Alyssa poked out her bottom lip. Why did he have to remind her?

"Do me a favor," her father said, directing her back toward the kitchen. "Stay out of the trees."

"What?" she asked, horrified. She was a monkey, a natural when it came to climbing. And she already had her mind set on a perch in her favorite Southern Red Oak tree, with her binoculars and a bag of Cheetos. "But I wanted to see the wedding."

"You can listen to it from your bedroom."

"Listen to it? That's not the same thing. You don't *listen* to a wedding. You *see* a wedding. You *experience* it."

Her father shook his head and remained firm. "You fell out of that oak tree last week and almost suffered a broken neck," he reminded her. "In case you haven't noticed, I have enough to worry about around here—like trying to feed twelve hundred guests."

Alyssa clamped her mouth shut.

"Promise me," he said.

She groaned, wishing he hadn't added that. What girl could resist watching a fairy-tale wedding in her own backyard? Didn't he know he was asking the impossible?

"Ally!" He stopped and spun her around by the shoulders. "Promise me," he insisted.

Alyssa sighed and dropped her head. "I promise," she mumbled, staring at her feet, all the while keeping her fingers crossed behind her back.

"Hmm. Something smells wonderful in here."

Alyssa and Alfred turned to see Quentin enter the kitchen and make a beeline toward one of the long silver trays.

Alyssa froze.

Quentin, Q as his friends called him, wasn't as tall as her father. But at six foot two, lean, and with a beautiful butterscotch complexion, it was no wonder women practically drooled whenever he was around.

Alyssa included.

"What's in here, Alfred?" Q asked, lifting a tray cover.

"Ah, ah, ah. Those lobster pot stickers are for the wedding."

Q quickly swiped one and plopped it in his mouth with a wink.

Alyssa stifled a giggle at his playful antics.

"Mr. Hinton, please," her father begged. "Everything must be perfect or Sterling will have my head on one of these silver platters."

When Q laughed, Alyssa thought it was the most beautiful sound on earth.

"Oh, loosen up, Alfred. Knowing you, everything will be *more* than perfect. Relax. Personally, I can't believe Jonas is crazy enough to give this whole marriage thing another try. Who knows? This time we might even reach the 'I do' part." Q laughed heartily and to Alyssa's amazement, his eyes landed on her.

"Oh, hello, Alice." He headed toward her.

Alyssa's eyes bugged and her tongue glued itself to the roof of her mouth.

"My, my. Aren't you a tall weed?" He looked her over. "How old are you now?"

She blinked while her mind went blank, mesmerized by his twinkling brown eyes.

After a lengthy silence, Quentin frowned. "Alfred, I think there's something wrong with your daughter. She's not a mute, is she?"

"No...um. She's shy."

"Oh." His gaze raked over her bony legs, flat chest and large eyes. "You better watch out for this one," he told Alfred. "She's going to break plenty of hearts when she grows up." He tweaked her right cheek. "Mine included," he added for her ears only.

Never!

"Don't I know it." Her father winked at her from

over Q's shoulder, oblivious to the youngest Hinton's teasing.

"There you are!" Sterling Hinton burst into the kitchen. "I've been looking all over the place for you."

Quentin swung his arm around Alyssa's shoulders before turning to face his older brother. "You know me. I can't stand to be apart from beautiful women."

Alyssa's face flushed with heat. *His arm is around my shoulder!*

"Don't you think Alyssa is a little *too* young for you?"

She frowned at Sterling. Who was he to rain on her parade?

"First of all," Q said, waving a finger, "her name is *Alice.* Second of all…well, there's no second."

"Have you been drinking?" Sterling asked, suspiciously.

"There's no law against it and it's well past noon. At least five minutes or so."

Fire lit behind Sterling's eyes and Alyssa cowered. Sterling didn't explode often. But when he did, watch out.

"If you ruin this day for Jonas—" Sterling seethed, jabbing a finger into the center of Q's chest "—I swear I'll kill you."

Q's arms fell from Alyssa's shoulders as he smiled in an attempt to tame a dragon. "I resent that. I was on my best behavior at Jonas's last wedding and I will be so again tonight. *But* if there's a third one, all bets are off."

"Smart-ass."

"Hey, hey. Watch the language in front of young Alice." Q looped his arm around his brother and directed him out of the kitchen. "The poor girl is painfully shy."

When the Hinton brothers disappeared from view of the kitchen, Alyssa's small shoulders slumped forward as her tongue finally unglued itself. "My name isn't Alice."

"Tough break, sweetheart." Her father tugged her fat pigtail. "At least this time he paid you a compliment."

"Some compliment."

"He basically said one day you'll be so beautiful you'll have your pick of any man, if my heart can take it. And the ones you don't choose will be heartbroken."

"Then I choose Quentin."

"Who knows? Maybe one day you'll have him." He sighed. "But you should keep your options open. Wide-open."

Alyssa knew her father didn't approve of Quentin—mainly because Q was a playboy—but he never came right out and discouraged her from her lofty dreams of marrying the man.

Yes, she knew what a playboy was. Being thirteen didn't mean she was naive. Besides, it didn't matter. When she grew up, Q would only have eyes for her. She would make sure of it.

A line of servers bowled through the kitchen's swinging doors and nearly knocked Alyssa over.

Her father cocked his head and gave her a pleading look.

"I'm going. I'm going," Alyssa said dejectedly and shuffled out of the kitchen with her head down. She headed out of the main house by the back door, hoping to catch one last look at the elaborate preparations.

Her frown wilted to an all-time low as she crept across the yard toward the servants' quarters. But, to get there, she had to pass her favorite oak tree. As she approached, a pair of male voices drifted on the afternoon air.

"Are you sure you're ready to do this again, son?"

Alyssa recognized her father's employer Roger Hinton's voice and she crouched down behind a line of shrubbery to eavesdrop.

"There won't be any surprises at this wedding, will there?"

"I can only hope not," Jonas joked with a nervous titter. "I think this time I picked someone who really wants to marry me."

"Good. Good," Mr. Hinton encouraged. "That's always a good strategy. Well, at any rate, I'm glad you chose to have the wedding here at the house. I can't tell you how much it means to your mother. Of course, she's hell-bent on getting the other two married off."

Jonas's gruff laughter rumbled around the men. "Good luck with Quentin. Mom might have to hog-tie him and drag him down the aisle."

"True. The boy is stubborn as a mule. He inherited that from your mother's side of the family."

Offended by the conversation about her future husband, Alyssa rolled her eyes. There was no one more hardheaded than Roger Hinton. A man who built a real estate empire by never accepting the word "no" and greasing a few pockets to make sure that he never would.

"You know, son, you never did tell me how you came to meet this new bride of yours."

"Didn't I?"

"No." A long puff of his cigar trailed his clipped response. "There's even talk around the house that she dated Sterling for a minute."

Alyssa's eyes widened at that revelation.

"I didn't know you listened to idle gossip, Dad."

"I've always found that there's a little truth to gossip and I have to say I'm mighty curious—me *and* your mother. Who is she? Where did she come from? And please tell me you had the bride sign a prenuptial agreement this time around. There are rumors you don't like those things, as well."

Jonas chuckled. "I'm not going to answer the prenuptial question, Dad. But it is sort of an interesting story about how Toni and I met…"

"Alyssa," Beatrice, the waiting staff supervisor called out at her, which gave away her position hiding behind the tree that shielded her from the Hintons.

Jonas peeked around the tree and grinned broadly down at her. "How long have you been down there?"

Alyssa's face reddened with embarrassment. "Not long," she lied.

Beatrice marched up to her like a wild twister in the middle of Oklahoma tornado season. "I have the staff setting up the buffet tables, do you mind helping me take the tea trays up to the bride's suite?"

Alyssa perked up. "Sure!" It was her first chance to get a good look at Jonas's future wife.

The family, as well as the staff, was surprised and curious about the woman who'd mended Jonas's heart and made him forget all about his former fiancée, Ophelia.

Alyssa and Beatrice loaded two serving carts and trekked to the east wing of the sprawling estate. As they approached the bride's suite, music and laughter spilled out into the hallway.

That magical buzz of excitement once again surrounded Alyssa and she couldn't wait to enter the room. The moment she did, it was like walking into Barbie's dream house. Beautiful women clustered together in different parts of the room. Some were getting their hair done, some getting their makeup done, and in the center stood the bride in a gorgeous, shoulderless, white gown.

The woman was practically glowing—and everyone knew why.

Alyssa sucked in a breath, convinced she'd never seen anything so beautiful in all her life—a real-life fairy-tale princess.

"Oh. The tea is here," one of the beautiful women in the bridal party exclaimed and rushed over to the carts.

"Tea?" a Spanish beauty quipped. "Please tell me there's something a little stronger than that on the cart."

"You're in luck," Beatrice said, reaching underneath the cart to the hidden second tray to pull out a bottle of champagne, chilling in a bucket of ice.

"Whoo. That's what I'm talking about!" The Spanish beauty grabbed the champagne. "Now, let's get this party started."

"Maria, you just make sure that you save some for the others," the bride warned.

"Don't be mad just because you can't have any. What? Are those butterflies finally kicking in, Toni? It's not too late to plan an escape route."

Alyssa's heart clutched. The idea of another bride ditching Jonas at the altar scared her.

"I'm not going anywhere," Toni said, holding still for last-minute alterations. "It took me forty-three years to find a man I wouldn't mind waking up to for the rest of my life."

"Who knew he was younger than you?"

"He's not that much younger…just seven years."

"Humph! Seven years means that he was in elementary school when you were graduating from high school," Maria said.

"And in elementary when you lost your virginity in the back of Jaron Miller's Hoopty," another woman added.

Alyssa quickly thought about the difference between her and Quentin's age.

"Ashley, there's a young lady in the room," Toni reminded her, and then smiled politely at Alyssa.

"Sorry," Ashley quipped.

"Aren't you a pretty little thing," Toni said.

Alyssa looked around to see if she was talking to someone else.

"I'm talking to you," the bride reassured. "How old are you?"

"T-thirteen."

"Ah, I remember thirteen," she said dreamily. "I received my first kiss at thirteen. Have you had your first kiss yet?"

Alyssa shook her head, but couldn't stop imagining a fantasy kiss with Quentin. He would pull her into his arms and…

"Aaah…so there *is* a boy you *want* to kiss," Toni said, reading her like an open book.

Alyssa dropped her gaze as her face heated.

All the women in the room noticed her reaction and chorused a long, "Awwwww…"

"Well, we should be getting back to the kitchen, Alyssa," Beatrice said.

"Alyssa. What a pretty name," the bride cooed. "Oh, can't she stay and help us around here?" Toni asked.

Beatrice hesitated.

"I'm sure my dad won't mind," Alyssa said before Beatrice could make up an excuse.

"Then that settles it. You can stay and hang out with us."

Beatrice's lips pressed into a hard, firm line and

her eyes flashed a warning to Alyssa to be on her best behavior before she backed out of the room.

"Alyssa, do you mind pouring my friends some tea?"

She shook her head and quickly went to work.

"So finish telling us how you snagged a ring from this young pup," another friend of the bride asked. "I want details."

Alyssa's ears perked up. She was eager to hear more about Jonas and Toni's love story. Who knows, maybe she would learn a few pointers.

"All right. Well, like I said I first started dating his brother…"

For an hour Alyssa remained rapt, caught up in Toni's version of events, but just when the story was getting really hot, the bride stopped talking. Then she slowly became aware that all eyes were on her.

"What? Did I do something wrong?"

Toni smiled and gathered up her dress so that she could glide over to her. "No, sweetheart. You haven't done anything wrong." She slid an arm around Alyssa's thin shoulders. "It's just that, uh, some of this story isn't fit for young ears."

The bridesmaids snickered softly behind them and Toni softened the blow by pinching Alyssa's apple cheeks.

"You mean that you want to talk about sex?" Alyssa asked.

"Well…" Toni looked around while her face darkened abruptly. "Something like that."

Alyssa's shoulders deflated as she dropped her head dramatically in hopes of convincing everyone to let her stay. When no one said a word, but instead let her cross the room slower than a turtle, she decided to offer a suggestion.

"You could always skip over the sex part."

"Not if she knows what's good for her," Ashley quipped.

"I know that's right," Maria agreed.

Brooklyn shook her head at her friends. "Behave."

"I'm sorry," Toni said again, this time poking out her bottom lip.

Defeated, Alyssa turned and walked out of the door. The minute she closed the door, peals of laughter erupted on the other side. "I can't wait until I grow up."

Another trickle of laughter slipped under the door, tempting Alyssa to press her ear against it to see if she could hear the rest of the story.

"Whatcha doing, Alice?"

Alyssa jumped and twirled away from the door. At the sight of her future husband strolling down the hallway, the muscles in her throat tightened and made it impossible for her speak.

Stopping in front of her, Quentin laughed and shook his head. "You know there's no need for you to be shy around me. You've been living here at my parents' home your whole life. We're practically family."

His words caused a world of butterflies to flutter madly in the pit of her stomach. She wanted to be a part of his family all right—the part that would marry him and give him at least a dozen babies that looked just like him.

The women laughed again; the melodic sound caught Q's ear. This time, he pressed his ear against the door but then winked down at her. A second later, he pulled away with a knowing smile.

"Oh, this isn't fit for young ears," he said, planting his hands on her shoulders and turning her away from the door. Alyssa sensed that if she wasn't there, he would have been more tempted to hang around and listen.

"We better find you something else to do," he said, laughing and directing her down the hallway. "If your father knew you were listening to that kind of stuff—"

"I wasn't," she said, finding her voice.

Q laughed. "Ah, so you do speak."

They reached the staircase and Alyssa's panic increased when she saw her father rushing around with the servers.

"Really," she insisted. "I just wanted to hear how the bride and groom fell in love. I didn't hear anything bad. Please don't tell my dad." She turned and glanced up at Quentin. "Please."

"Alyssa?" Her father called.

She turned and smiled down at him. "Hey, Dad."

"Is there a problem?" His suspicious gaze darted from her to Quentin.

"No, sir. I just finished helping the bride and the bridesmaids."

Alfred nodded, but his eyes remained locked on the youngest Hinton. "All right, then. You go on to your room and try to stay out of the way."

"Yes, sir." She started down the staircase, but relaxed when she heard Q's soft whisper.

"Don't worry. It will be our little secret."

Alyssa was supposed to go to her room.

She always had a hard time doing what she was told—especially now that the guests had started to arrive. Beautiful women draped on the arms of handsome men had her young, romantic mind churning and her body itching to be a part of the festivities.

Maybe she could.

The moment the possibility crossed her mind, her shoulders deflated when the promise she made her father floated through her mind.

"Cheer up, Alice. Things can't be all that bad."

Alyssa's head jerked up to see Quentin leaning against the oak door, leading to the service quarters. Her heart flip-flopped in her chest and when he flashed his dimpled cheeks, she nearly swooned on the spot. "What are you doing here?"

Q shrugged. "Well, if you don't want me here, I'm sure I can find a group of females who'd actually enjoy my company." He pushed away from the door and started to head back toward the wedding party. "I just thought you wanted to hear the rest of Jonas and Toni's story. Silly me."

"Wait." She raced over to him and grabbed him by the wrist. "I do."

When he turned to face her, she was suddenly stunned by her own behavior and released his hand while embarrassment scorched her entire body.

"Ah. So you are interested?"

She was much more interested in spending time with him.

He laughed. "What is it about women that makes them love sappy love stories?"

Women? Did he consider her a woman now?

Alyssa straightened and even tried to thrust up her flat chest. Her effort wrangled another laugh from him. "Calm down." He tugged her fat pigtail. "Don't try to grow up so fast, sport. You have plenty of time to torture the opposite sex, Alice."

She smiled, enjoying their budding friendship. "It's Alyssa," she said meekly.

"What?"

"My name." She shrugged. "It's Alyssa—not Alice."

"Alyssa," he repeated. His eyes sparkled like diamonds. "I like it."

Another flash of his dimples and her knees nearly folded.

"Now about this story." He leaned back against the door. "I can't tell you all of it, but if you tell me where you left off, I can tell you what I do know."

For another half hour, Alyssa listened intently to more of Jonas and Toni's love story before they were rudely interrupted.

"Q!" Sterling shouted and stormed toward his startled brother. "There you are. I've been looking all over the place for you."

"Well then, mission accomplished, dear bro." Quentin made a mock bow and then winked over at Alyssa. "If I'm not careful, one of these days they're going to implant a Lojack device under my skin and I'll never be able to sneak off with you again."

To her surprise, an uncharacteristic giggle tumbled from her lips. It was what other women did whenever they were around Quentin—not that she was a woman, yet. But soon, she promised herself, she would be.

Belatedly, Sterling noticed the starry-eyed teenager. Suspicion narrowed in his eyes as his gaze ping-ponged between the two. "Am I interrupting something?"

Q took one look at his brother's face and launched one eyebrow high along his forehead. "Certainly not what you're thinking."

Sterling cleared his throat while looking both guilty and embarrassed.

Alyssa wasn't sure she followed the conversation.

"I was simply filling little *Alyssa* in on how our wonderful brother Jonas has, once again, found himself ready to walk the plank into the abyss of happily—ever—after."

Sterling's gaze fell to the empty champagne glass in his brother's hand. "How many of those have you had?"

"Not nearly enough," Q laughed. "But hey, the night is still young." This time he winked at his older brother.

Sterling drew a deep breath in an obvious effort to remain calm. "Dad wants to see you. He's in his library." He glanced at his watch. "When you're done, Jonas wants to see you."

"Well, I guess I shouldn't keep them waiting," Q said, marching away.

Disappointed, Alyssa's shoulders slumped at having been so quickly forgotten. Then, as if he'd heard her thoughts, Q stopped and turned with a magnanimous smile.

"Oh, but I haven't finished telling poor little Alice the story."

Alice again.

Once again, Sterling's gaze shifted to the shy tomboy.

"Don't worry." Q smiled. "I was real careful to omit the racy parts. Perhaps you could finish for me?"

Horror rippled across Sterling Hinton's face like he wasn't quite used to talking to someone so young.

"Don't worry," Q continued. "She won't bite." He made a silent toast with his empty champagne glass and stalked off.

Alyssa smiled dreamily after her future husband until he disappeared into the house. A sigh, she didn't even realize she was holding, exploded from her chest.

Sterling chuckled.

Embarrassed, Alyssa's face heated to the point her cheeks felt like they were on fire.

"I've seen that look before," Sterling said, with an air of superiority that irked Alyssa. She didn't like it—not even for a moment—that she'd given her emotions away to a man who would undoubtedly feel it was his duty to give her some type of speech.

"Don't worry," he covered. "Your secret is safe with me."

Unable to hide her surprise, Alyssa eyed Sterling with wary and cautious eyes.

"What?" he asked innocently enough. "I know what it's like to have a crush."

It took everything she had not to protest and proclaim what she felt for Quentin was stronger than any schoolgirl crush. Q was her destiny.

"Or maybe I should say what it feels like to be in love?"

Alyssa experienced another jolt of surprise. Somehow the man was truly reading her thoughts.

Sterling smiled and for a brief moment, his handsome good looks rivaled his younger brother and she was stunned by how it sent her heart aflutter.

"I better get back to my room," she said, and turned toward to the servants' quarters.

"You don't want to hear the rest of the story?"

Surprised, she stopped in her tracks. "You don't mind telling me?"

"Well, I'm sure I'm not as colorful a storyteller as Q…but if you really want to know."

Alyssa faced him again to judge whether he was being sincere or just being charitable.

"Where did you guys leave off?"

She hesitated, but when she realized that he was

being sincere, she approached. "Jonas kicked Ms. Wright out of his condo after she tried to break things off."

"Well that is the PC version of things," he chuckled.

Alyssa frowned and Sterling cleared his throat.

"Well, let's just say that Jonas refused to speak to Toni after that." Sterling continued the story and concluded when Jonas finally proposed to his pregnant girlfriend. It was truly a romantic story that had Alyssa casting herself in Toni's role and Quentin in Jonas's role. Alyssa sighed. The story had a happy ending—just the way she liked it. Now, here she was at the center of what would undoubtedly be dubbed a fairy-tale wedding…and she had to stay in her room.

"Fifteen minutes to showtime," the wedding planner said as she rushed by, alerting the wedding party. "Everyone take their places."

Sterling smiled and stood up straight. "I guess that means me, too." His gaze raked over her attire: blue jeans, Mary J. Blige T-shirt and a pair of Reeboks that had seen better days. "I know I'm long past being hip. Well, I was never what you would call hip…but is that what you're wearing to the wedding?"

Alyssa dropped her head and couldn't help but poke out her bottom lip. "I can't go. Dad said that I would just be in the way."

Sterling chuckled and then placed a comforting arm around her shoulders. "Nonsense." He looked her over again. "It just so happens that I require a date for this evening. How fast can you change clothes?"

Hope bloomed in Alyssa's heart. "But Daddy said—"

"I'll have a talk with Alfred. I'm sure I can get him to change his mind."

"Do you really think so?"

Sterling's chest swelled with confidence. "I'm a pretty persuasive guy. It's served me well in business."

"Yeah, but—"

"Trust me."

He winked and again Alyssa was charmed by his uncharacteristic playful side. "Okay," she said backing away. "I'll go change." She turned and raced off to her room. The only dress she had in her closet suitable for a wedding was the frilly number her father bought her for Easter. She frowned at the excessive lace, but quickly showered and shimmied into the dress in what had to be an Olympic record.

A couple of brush strokes through her hair, a ribbon and she was out the door. As she rushed to grab one of the white, wooden lawn chairs she took in the final staging for the ceremony and felt as if she had been cast into a glorious dream. White and pink flowers were strewn as far as the eye could see while a live orchestra played as if they were introducing her to the crowd.

No sooner had she found a seat on the groom's side, than someone handed her a folded letter. She suspected it was from her father before she even opened it.

And she was right.

Be on your *best* behavior.
—Dad

Alyssa smiled and folded the letter. Sterling had pulled off a miracle and she would be eternally grateful.

A handsome Jonas took his place before the preacher, looking happy *and* nervous. The processional music started up and everyone turned in their seats in time to see the first bridesmaid and groomsman march down the aisle.

Of course, Alyssa's heart didn't start pounding until Quentin appeared, escorting a blushing Maria. Alyssa pretended not to notice the subtle signs of the beautiful Latina flirting with her future husband. Q spotted Alyssa in the crowd and winked.

In that moment, if she had died, she would have left this world the happiest girl alive.

I will marry you one day, Quentin Dwayne Hinton. I will.

Sterling was the next Hinton to walk down the aisle. When he, too, spotted her in her silly Easter dress, he smiled and gave her the thumbs-up. She smiled and mouthed the words *thank you*.

The wedding march began and everyone rose to their feet when the bride marched down the aisle on the arm of her friend Isaiah Washington. She was six months pregnant and glowed like the sun. When everyone returned to their seats, they all waited in anticipation for the "I do's."

This time, neither the bride nor groom stopped the wedding. Precisely twenty minutes later, the minister introduced Mr. and Mrs. Hinton to the wedding guests.

The fairy-tale wedding wasn't over for Alyssa. To her surprise, Q offered his arm for her first dance. Being in his arms was like a dream come true and it took everything she had not to make a fool of herself.

"Ah, I still stand by my earlier assessment," he said. "One day, you *will* break men's hearts. I just pray I won't be one of them."

She was sure her entire body turned beet-red and it was a wonder that she didn't trip all over his feet.

However, when the song ended, Quentin disappeared to sweep another woman off her feet.

"May I?" Sterling asked.

"Yes, you may." Alyssa glided into his arms and soon discovered he was as good a dancer as his younger brother. "Thank you for talking my dad into letting me attend."

"Oh, think nothing of it. What else are friends for?"

She smiled, feeling for the first time that she was his friend and not just some servant's daughter. Alas the dance ended too quickly and Sterling disappeared into the crowd, as well.

"My. My. My. Aren't you popular with the Hinton men," an attractive woman in a stunning aqua-blue gown whispered. "If you were a little older, I'm willing to bet half the eligible women here would be plotting to scratch your eyes out."

Alyssa giggled, liking the idea of women being jealous of her. Especially those who thought they actually had a chance with her man. "They're welcome to try," she whispered back.

It was the woman's turn to giggle. "I like you, little girl. You have spunk."

It wasn't spunk, Alyssa knew. She had a plan.

Chapter 1

The Dollhouse, Atlanta, Georgia

This was the last place Quentin wanted to be.

The alcohol wasn't so bad. It was the loud crowd and his obnoxious friends that were grating on his nerves, a first since he'd dedicated most of his life to partying and seducing beautiful women. Now he was off his game.

Way off.

"You sorry son of a bitch!" Some guy who didn't like Quentin putting the moves on his girl grabbed Quentin's shoulder and spun him around and then crashed his fist solidly against his jaw.

Pain exploded in Quentin's head as he crumpled

to the floor. The sad part was that he welcomed it. Anything was better than the frosty numbness of the past three days.

"C'mon. Get up so I can kick your ass!" the man shouted, his breath strong enough to singe his nose hairs.

Q's friends parted like the Red Sea while lap dancers screeched and ran out of the way to avoid the fight.

"Get up!"

"C'mon, man. Is all this worth it?" Q struggled to his feet. He casually dusted himself off, and then was careful not to meet anyone's eyes as he licked the trickle of blood from the corner of his lips. Around him, friends and strangers gawked and waited to see what would happen next. He rather hoped the next blow would render him unconscious for a few days. "The chick wasn't even all that good-looking."

"Oh, you got jokes." The man launched toward Q, but thankfully his best friend, and co-Dollhouse owner, Xavier King, jumped into the mix.

"Whoa. Whoa. I just finished remodeling the place. Y'all want to fight, take it to Caesar's Palace or something."

Xavier, a former heavyweight champion with arms that felt like steel bands, successfully dragged the drunkard back a few inches from Quentin's cowed position on the floor. "Let it go. Let it go."

Q's laugh rumbled, but the notes were depressingly sad. "Nah. Nah. Bring it on. I can take him."

It was Q's cockiness that goaded the man's temper and gave him the strength of ten men to break Xavier's hold. Once he got loose all hell broke loose. There were plenty of screams. Friends and strangers jumped in for no reason at all. Bouncers and security guards tangled and before anyone knew it, there were gunshots popping off in the club.

Q experienced firsthand what it was like to be a defenseless punching bag while receiving blow after blow. The man was really trying his best to permanently rearrange Quentin's face, and was doing a damn good job of it, too. To his utter dismay, it took a few dozen solid punches before a black curtain closed over this hellish reality. When he finally woke, a stern-looking Hispanic man crouched over him flashing a penlight into his eyes, which caused a near explosion in the back of his head.

He croaked out a miserable groan and raised an arm up to shield his eyes. "What the hell, man? Are you trying to kill me?"

"Looks like he's gonna live," the man's heavily accented voice announced.

It should have been good news, but Quentin didn't receive it as such. In fact, it was the worst news he could have received.

"Sir, how are you feeling? We have an ambulance outside. Would you like to go to the hospital?"

Quentin shrugged from the man's touch and then waved him off.

"Suit yourself," the paramedic said, turned and left Q where he sat on the floor.

A second later another set of footsteps strolled over to him. A large hand jutted out in front of his face. "Finished bleeding on my floor?"

Q tried to broker a smile, but it hurt too damn much. Putting his pride aside, he slid his hand into his cousin's and was grateful that with one firm jerk he was back onto his feet. Now all he had to do was stay on them. He didn't look directly at Xavier, but squinting his eyes around the periphery, he saw his best friend looking around and shaking his head. Following Xavier's lead, he took in the scene himself, or at least he tried to with eyes that were ready to swell shut. The crowds were gone and the club was apparently closed. It looked like a wrecking ball had leveled the place.

"Aww, man. Sorry about this."

"Sorry?" Xavier snapped, his tone nearly the same decibel as a roaring lion. "Sorry doesn't fix our crib." He drew in a few deep breaths and seemingly regained control of himself.

"Here you go, boss." One of the female employees approached and handed him something before flashing Quentin a sympathetic smile and then sauntering off. The old Quentin would have followed up an open invitation like that. The new Quentin wanted to stay the hell away from women.

Far away.

"Man, I've never seen anyone get their ass handed to them like that since the Tyson-Holyfield fight,"

Xavier said, wincing and handing over a handmade ice pack. Since he was Quentin's favorite cousin, he felt free to make such a flippant remark. "I might be mistaken, but I think that brother was trying to reconstruct your face." He chuckled, a clear sign he was getting over his anger.

"Very funny," Q mumbled, limping his way. He tilted his bruised and bloody head back and put the ice pack back on his throbbing temple. This must be what it felt like to be run over by a Mack truck.

"I wasn't trying to be funny." Xavier stepped back. "And don't drip blood on my shoes." He snickered and followed his cousin over to the nearest bar. He walked around the counter and grabbed two glasses.

Q moaned and groaned about his injuries.

"You know you could have blocked a few of those punches," Xavier said. "Haven't you ever heard of stick and move?"

"You're not helping."

Xavier shook his head. "Seriously. What's up with you? You haven't been yourself for a while. We either need to talk this out or I'm going to have to ban you from coming in here."

"I'm part owner."

"I know. Awkward, huh?"

Q snorted.

"I'm waiting."

"It's about this…woman."

"Now why aren't I surprised?" Xavier's laughter exploded, shaking his entire frame.

"Trust me. She's not just any woman." Quentin sighed, lowered the ice pack.

Xavier winced and twisted his face as if he was viewing a crime scene. "Put that back on. And you might want to reconsider calling a doctor. That nose is going to need some serious reconstructive work."

Q moaned but did as his best friend suggested. The ice pack felt good against his tight, throbbing skin anyway.

"What can I get you?" asked Xavier.

"I'll have what you're having," Q croaked. "But make it a double."

Xavier filled the second glass to the rim with good old reliable Jack Daniel's. "I think I'll leave the bottle out," he said. "It looks likes you're gonna need it."

Quentin agreed.

Xavier turned away briefly to put away some glasses, but by the time he turned back, Q had already emptied his first shot glass.

"Whoever this chick is, she's done one hell of a number on you." Xavier said, shaking his head as if he couldn't fathom such a thing. "I've never seen you like this and I've seen you with plenty of women."

Quentin didn't respond. Instead he reached for the Jack Daniel's bottle himself and refilled his glass.

"Since we had to close early tonight *and* you don't seem to be in any hurry to go home, why don't you tell me about this mysterious woman that's worth you getting your ass whooped over?"

Silence.

"Well, what's her name?"

There was another long pause, and then, "Alyssa," Q said more to his empty glass than his cousin. "But I call her Alice…"

A Diamond in Plain Sight

Chapter 2

Six years earlier...

"Beautiful!" Emmanuel shouted while clicking away with his 35 mm camera. "Now tilt your head just a little more to the right."

Expertly, Alyssa followed the renowned photographer's direction with effortless ease and grace. It had taken years to master holding a bright or even sexy smile while frolicking on a beach in freezing weather.

"Aw. That's it. That's it," Emmanuel praised. "Give me a little more shoulder. Yes. Yes. Beautiful." It was the second time Alyssa and the celebrity photographer had worked together and just like before, both experienced a wonderful chemistry that was raw and unique in such a hard, jaded business.

A wicked chill raced down Alyssa's spine, but with steel determination, she kept her teeth from chattering. Though her modeling had taken her all over the world, this was her first photo shoot on Paradise Beach in beautiful Mykonos, Greece. She could just do without the late fall weather.

"All right. Take ten," Emmanuel shouted, and then gave Alyssa an encouraging wink.

The crew broke into immediate applause. The men, both gay and straight, showered her with praise while the women were polite but a bit standoffish. All in all, it was the way the business operated. Ever since Alyssa first began her modeling career, people approached her with their own preconceptions of what she was all about: shallow, vapid and vain. Nothing could have been further from the truth.

Alyssa popped out of the water and welcomed the large towel offered to her by one of the assistants like it was a life jacket. In many ways it was. It had become impossible to stop her teeth from clacking together.

"You were wonderful," the young assistant assured her. "Everyone is going to be buzzing about these photos when they come out. No doubt you'll get the cover of Sports Illustrated this year."

"Thanks," Alyssa said. She'd made the highly coveted cover last year and was just pleased to have been asked again to pose. Still, there was no denying that the cover had accelerated her already rising modeling career and despite shoots like this, she loved every moment of it.

"Here. This should be better." Tangela, Alyssa's best friend and solo entourage, raced over with a warm bulky coat she'd kept near a portable heater and draped it around Alyssa's shoulders.

"Aww. Tangie, you're the best." Alyssa said, closing her eyes in near ecstasy.

"Just doing my job, taking care of you."

Thank God, Alyssa thought. She honestly believed that her life would've been much harder without at least *one* person she could trust unconditionally— one person that wasn't jealous of her success.

Alyssa and Tangela walked behind the tracking lights and ignored the buffet table, loaded down with high calories and sugary temptations. As usual, her stomach growled loudly in protest.

"Oh, I brought some carrots," Tangela offered. "You want some?"

Carrots. How appetizing. Her stomach gave another long winding growl and Alyssa quickly realized that something was better than nothing. "Give me the carrots."

Tangela, as always, laughed at Alyssa's diet grumpiness and quickly rummaged through her knapsack for the boring, crunchy snack while Alyssa's ears perked at the sound of something ringing.

"Do you hear that?"

Tangela looked up. "Hear what?"

Riiiinnng.

"Oh. Your cell phone is in the coat pocket," Tanglea said.

Alyssa shoved her hands into her pockets and scooped out her BlackBerry. She read the ID screen and smiled. "Hello, Daddy."

"Hey, baby girl. How are you? I didn't catch you at a bad time, did I?" he asked gruffly.

"There's never a bad time for you," she said and meant it. Despite the distance and her fewer and fewer visits home, they had a close and special relationship. In fact, she considered him more of a best friend than her girl, Tangela. "So what's up?"

Tangela held out the small bag of carrots and Alyssa reached over and grabbed a few.

"Well, I was wondering if you were free this weekend?"

Alyssa frowned at the question. "Well, I don't know, I'd have to check my calendar. Why, is something up?" She chomped down on her carrot and pretended that it was a piping hot, glazed doughnut. When her father didn't immediately answer, her hackles rose. Was there something wrong? Was he sick? "Dad?" Her heartbeat quickened. What would she do if something happened to him? He was the only family she had.

"Actually, baby girl…I'm getting married."

Silence.

"Ally? Are you there?"

She blinked, swallowed and choked on that pesky carrot.

"Ally?"

Dropping the phone, tears surfaced and streamed, sufficiently ruining Alyssa's makeup.

Tangela sprang into action and started whacking Alyssa on the back. "Are you all right?"

Married? Did he just say that he was getting married? Feeling her spine about to snap in half, Alyssa flailed her hands to ward her friend off. "All right. All right. I'm okay."

"You're supposed to chew before you swallow," Tangela said as if she needed reminding.

"My phone. Where is my phone?" Alyssa glanced around and spotted it in the white sand and snatched it up.

"Ally? Ally? Are you still there?"

"Yeah, I'm here." She moved away from Tangela, trying to figure out what to say. "Um, this is um…wow."

Her father chuckled. "I know this may come as a surprise."

That's an understatement. "I didn't even know that you were seeing anyone," she admitted and tried to ignore her bruised feelings. "Anyone I know?"

"Well, yeah. I, um, you met her long time ago. Estelle Sullivan."

Alyssa shook her head, not placing a face to the name.

"She, um, used to teach at Springfield Elementary."

The name suddenly clicked. "Ms. Sullivan—my second grade teacher?"

"See. I knew you'd remember her." His voice perked with pride.

Alyssa glanced back over her shoulder at Tangie, who in turn, mouthed the inquiry, "What's wrong?"

My father has lost his mind, she wanted to say.

"So, do you think you'll be able to come? Mister Hinton said that we could have the wedding right here on the property. After that, well, I'm retiring."

Whoa. This was a lot of new information at one time. How long had she been trying to get her father to quit his job as the Hintons' personal chef?

"Baby girl?"

"Uh, yeah," she said, still struggling with the proper way to respond. "Well, wow. This is *big* news. Really big."

"It is," he admitted. "But I gotta tell you…it's been a long time since I've been this happy. This…complete."

Alyssa closed her eyes at the raw emotion she heard in her father's voice.

"I love her, baby girl."

Her smile returned. "Then I love her, too, Dad."

"So does that mean that you'll come?"

"It means that I wouldn't miss it for the world."

"A paper, please," Quentin said, walking up to one of the many New York newsstands in the middle of Times Square.

"Which one," the brusque vendor asked, gesturing toward a variety.

"Times," Q answered, shoving his hand into his pants pocket to dig around for some change, but from the corners of his eyes a magazine cover caught his attention. He turned his head and leaned forward. The tall beauty that stared back at him from the glossy page had the effect of a steel punch to the gut. He couldn't remember ever seeing a woman with such magnetic and soulful eyes—and those curves and long limbs. *Good Lord, have mercy!*

The vendor cleared his throat.

Q jumped and returned his attention to the man.

"Will there be anything else?" he asked.

"No." Quentin shook his head. There was no way he was about to buy *Vogue.* He didn't want to give the vendor the wrong idea. He paid for his paper but before strolling off he gave the magazine a quick final glance. Minutes later, he arrived at his favorite morning eatery, Diamond Dairy. Not surprising, his brother Sterling was already there and waiting for him.

"Would it hurt you to be late for something once in your life?" Q asked, plopping into the chair across from his brother.

"Would it hurt you to be *on time* for something once in your life?" Sterling volleyed without blinking an eye.

"Now why in the world would I want to do something like that?"

"Morning, boys." Tabitha, their usual waitress, greeted them with a piping hot coffee pot. "What will it be?"

"The usual, Tabby," Q answered, as he peeled open his newspaper. He went straight for the crossword puzzle and pulled out a pen from his pocket.

"Same here," Sterling said, and retrieved the rest of the paper. "I don't know how you can do that thing. I can never get more than a couple of answers."

"That's because *I'm* the genius in the family," Q taunted. Years ago, to everyone's disbelief, Quentin had scored a 170 on his IQ test, higher than both his brothers, who were successful in business—a fact that he never let anyone forget.

Sterling shook his head and fingered his tie. "Too bad that you don't use that big brain of yours to get a job."

"C'mon. Not that again. I got a job once, remember? After we got Jonas hitched to Toni. I put in my six months at Hinton Enterprises and now I'm on vacation."

"That was *years* ago."

"And I'm still traumatized."

Sterling laughed and shook his head. "I called you this morning."

Q's eyebrows crawled up his forehead. "Oh?"

"New girlfriend?"

"Change the subject," Quentin said. "You know I never kiss and tell."

"Since when?"

"Since now."

"But aren't you supposed to be—I thought you and Dad had made a deal?" When Quentin didn't answer, Sterling shook his head. "I swear. You'll never change."

"That's the goal," Q boasted.

"Well, try not to hit on any of the bridesmaids this weekend. It would be considered bad form."

"What are you talking about?"

"Mom didn't call you?"

Tabitha returned and placed two western omelets in front of the brothers.

"What, is Mom seeing a new psychic or something?" Q asked, grabbing his fork.

"No. Alfred is getting married this weekend." Sterling sipped at his coffee. "And we've been invited."

"Get out of here!" Q laughed. "Alfred's jumping the broom? That old dog!"

Q exhaled and pushed back in his chair. "Jeez, I haven't been home in a long time."

Sterling's smile returned. "Yep. He's a good man. I'm happy for him." He took another sip of his coffee. "It's good to find love at any age."

"Guess that means you can hit the senior circuit and pick yourself up a wife before she wheels away."

Sterling scowled. "I'm only a year older than you."

"But you act twenty years older."

"Not funny."

Q snickered and then spotted a woman at the next table, holding up *Vogue* magazine. The cover model pulled at him again. Why did that face seem so familiar?

"What is it?" Sterling glanced around to see what caught Quentin's attention.

"Nothing," Q assured him with a shake of his head. "My mind is just playing tricks on me." What else could it be? Surely, he couldn't have known the woman on the cover of *Vogue*. No way he could've *ever* forgotten such a face.

Chapter 3

"Baby girl, you made it!" Alfred threw open his arms as his daughter raced from her luxury rental car and flashed him with her million-dollar smile—her mother's smile. When her slight weight pressed against him, he wrapped his long thick arms around her and rocked her from side to side in his exuberance. "I'm so happy to see you."

Alyssa eased back to look into her father's eyes. "You look so good."

Her father's smile brightened. "That's because my favorite girl has finally come home. Everyone is waiting for you inside." He released her from his embrace. "Let me help you get your bags." Alfred rushed over to the trunk of her car. "Oh hey, Tangela."

He gave the young woman a quick hug, as well. "I'll get those for you," he said, taking the luggage from her hands.

"Thank you, Mr. Jansen."

"Don't mention it." Alfred loaded his arms with their luggage and escorted them to Alyssa's old bedroom in the servants' quarters.

"I don't believe it," Alyssa said, looking around. "You haven't changed a thing." The thought both surprised and pleased her. Her gaze took in the soft pastels, the Laura Ashley collection, and the hundreds of stuffed animals she'd collected over the years. It was truly like stepping back in time.

"It's your room. It never felt right packing any of this stuff up," her father said, setting the luggage down.

"But you're going to be leaving the Hinton estate soon, aren't you, Mr. Jansen?" Tangela asked. "You and your new wife aren't going to continue to live here."

Alfred shook his head. "No…we, um, bought a place in Atlanta."

"*Atlanta*?" Alyssa and Tangela echoed.

Alfred nodded. "Estelle has some family there."

He's marrying into a whole new family? "That's nice," Alyssa lied.

Her father walked over and draped his arms around her small shoulders. "Don't give me that look. My marrying Estelle doesn't mean I'm going to stop being your father. Nothing will ever stop that."

Alyssa wasn't embarrassed by her jealousy. "I know that."

"Good." Her father pressed his lips against her right temple. "Now what do you say we head on over to the kitchen where I can whip you girls up something to eat? You need to put a little more meat on those bones."

"Well, actually—"

"Don't tell me you're on another crazy diet," her father said. "There's a no-diet rule when you come to see me, remember?"

Tangela looked as though she was ready to kiss him. "Then we need to visit you more often," she joked.

Laughing, Alfred escorted the ladies toward the main house, while describing a mouth-watering clam and mussels dish. When he had finished, both Alyssa and Tangela's stomachs growled in unison.

"Oh my God! Alyssa, is that you?"

Before she could turn all the way around, Alyssa was crushed in a pair of strong arms. "I can't believe it. Let me get a good look at you!" The woman stepped back, holding Alyssa's shoulders at arm's length.

"Ms. Beatrice," Alyssa declared, beaming a radiant smile at the older woman. "How good it is to see you." There were considerably more wrinkles in the woman's kind face and her once salt-and-pepper hair was now completely cotton-ball white.

"Stunning," Beatrice praised. "Absolutely stunning." Her arms looped around Alyssa's waist. "Didn't I tell you that you'd fill out one day? I bet you can hardly get the men off you. How many are you juggling? Two? Five? Twenty? I want details."

Alfred cleared his throat. "I'm still standing here, you know."

The women laughed.

Alfred shook his head and turned toward his stove.

Beatrice herded Alyssa and Tangela toward the long servants' table at the end of the gigantic kitchen. "I want to hear everything," she insisted. "The glamorous life of a supermodel."

"I don't know about glamorous, but it's certainly hectic."

"The parties are fun, though," Tangela tossed in. "Whenever I can get Alyssa to go."

"Still a homebody, eh?" Beatrice said with a note of disappointment. "Honey, if I was you, I'd be living it up before those perky breasts head south and that small waist of yours expands."

Again, Alfred cleared his throat.

"Don't even pretend that you don't know what I mean," Beatrice chided. "Or you wouldn't be marrying someone fifteen years younger than you."

Alfred fell silent.

Alyssa and Tangela shared a look. Clearly Beatrice disapproved of Alfred's engagement.

"Well, I think love knows no age," Alyssa said, standing up for her father. "All that matters is how two people feel toward each other."

"So tell me," Beatrice said, returning her attention to Alyssa. "Stop stalling. Talk."

Suddenly tongue-tied, Alyssa shrugged. The image of her supermodel job didn't exactly match up with reality. Before she could start playing catch-up, the kitchen door swung open. Jamie and Lidi, the estate's two maids, entered, trailed by James, the gardener, and Antonio, the butler.

"There she is!" Jamie shouted.

"I told you I saw them pull up," James exclaimed.

Alyssa was instantly surrounded and pulled from one embrace to another. Everyone marveled and praised her for how much she'd transformed from the skinny knock-kneed little girl who raced around the estate and climbed everything that stood still.

"Oooh. I can't wait until Quentin gets a good look at you," Lidi cooed. "You'll finally have him eating out of the palm of your hand."

Jamie and Beatrice elbowed her.

"What?" Lidi asked, innocently.

Alyssa perked up. "Q's coming?"

"Oooh, there's that look," Lidi said, smiling. "I told you she still had a thing for him."

"No. That's not true," Alyssa said. "I was just curious."

"Even I don't buy that one," her father said, pouring white wine into the pot of heated olive oil.

"No. I mean it," she insisted. "I know I used to have a *minor* crush on him, but that was years ago. I've outgrown it."

"Minor?" Beatrice barked as her whole body

shook with mirth. "That's putting it mildly. Anytime he came home, you sneaked around the property like Nancy Drew."

"I did not," Alyssa lied, feeling her face flush with embarrassment.

"I caught you crawling around the main library when he was in there once," Beatrice reminded her.

"And I discovered you climbing the trellis outside his bedroom a couple of times," James chimed.

Alfred looked up from chopping garlic. "What?"

"Mr. James!" Alyssa gasped.

"I—I wasn't trying to look into Q's room," Alyssa stammered. "Billy Dee Williams had climbed up on the roof that time. Don't you remember, Mr. James?" She widened her eyes and mentally willed him to play along.

James laughed. "I've never known of any of Mrs. Hinton's pampered Chihuahuas climbing up the roof."

Traitor.

"What about the time you stole away in the trunk of the limo?" Antonio asked. "You said that you were going to sneak into Quentin's luggage and fly with him on one of his trips. Now *that* was hilarious. I think Mr. Sterling found you that time."

"Alyssa!" her father snapped. "Tell me you didn't."

"Thanks guys for ratting me out," Alyssa said, rolling her eyes. "My Christmas list is going to be a lot shorter this year."

"Aww. You know we love you," Antonio said, kissing her on the cheek and stealing another hug.

"We just aren't buying that you're really over Mister Quentin."

"Yeah," Beatrice added. "I'll believe *that* when I see it."

Quentin slept during the flight to South Carolina. It was either do that or drink every one of those cute little bottles the airline attendant had stocked on the flight. That was always the choice when flying back to his parents' estate—or more to the point, when it came to seeing his father. Luckily these visits were few and far between.

The problem was that he and his father never saw eye to eye. Usually when they spent time together, one could set their watch by how long it would take before they were embroiled in a heated argument. No doubt this trip wouldn't be any different, especially now that he'd struck a deal with the devil.

The moment the airplane touched down, Quentin opened his eyes and stretched in his seat.

"Welcome back to the living," Sterling said, pulling out his BlackBerry from his breast pocket. "I had to endure quite a few complaints about your snoring while you were knocked out."

"I'm sure you were able to handle things like you always do," Quentin answered, unfazed. "Why else do you think I keep you around?"

"I wonder about that myself," Sterling said, cracking a half smile.

Quentin turned his head and noticed a woman

across the aisle clutching the current issue of *Vogue*. Good Lord, was that magazine stalking him?

The plane rolled slowly up to the gate and minutes later the passengers jumped out of their seats and popped open the overhead bins. After bumping into bodies and joining in the mass exodus, Sterling and Quentin made their way toward baggage claim.

Before they reached their destination, Antonio, their father's lifelong driver, stood before baggage claim with a placard that read: HINTONS.

"Mister Quentin and Mister Sterling," Antonio greeted. "How wonderful it is to see you."

"Likewise, my man," Sterling returned, slapping a hand against the man's back. "Imagine my surprise that Alfred is actually going to beat you back down the aisle."

"What can I say?" Antonio said, blushing. "He got lucky."

The men laughed and then saw to the bags getting loaded into the limo.

"Do you know if Jonas and Toni are flying in?" Quentin asked, leaning toward the minibar.

Sterling frowned as he once again pulled out a stack of papers from his briefcase to work on during their ride to the estate. "They're flying in on Saturday morning."

"Good. Good. I haven't seen them since Jonas packed up his company and shipped them out to Georgia."

"They have planes that fly to Georgia, too, you know."

"Yeah, but I don't want Jonas thinking that I'm finished with my vacation so he can put me back to work."

"Issues." Sterling buried his face into his paperwork once again. "I may be moving back to my Atlanta office myself. I need a slower pace for a while."

"Fine. I guess I'll have to come visit *both* of you."

Quentin finished pouring his drink and then settled back in his seat. "I *am* going to work one of these days…as soon as I settle on the career I'd like to pursue. You always said that I should pursue something I enjoy."

"You mean now that your days of being a gigolo are over?"

"I prefer the term *connoisseur of women*," he said, smiling and then glancing out of the window. "It takes a special kind of man to really appreciate women—the incredible artistry God creates in the curve of a woman's hip, the size, weight and warmth of a good, firm breast. And their scent…" He swirled the amber liquid in his glass and remained thoughtful. "Did you know that every woman has their own unique scent?"

Sterling glanced up from his papers.

"It's true," Quentin insisted. "It's faint, buried beneath their perfume, soft baby powder and fruity lotions. But it's there and it's intoxicating—every one of them."

"Well, I'll be damn," Sterling sighed. "You're a poet."

"Connoisseur," Quentin repeated. "And damn proud of it.

"I don't know how I'm going to survive this arrangement. Monogamy is not in my DNA."

Minutes later, the limo turned onto the Hinton estate. A sea of lush green grass surrounded the long spiraling driveway. Quentin caught sight of two women out by the stables. Though he couldn't identify who they were, his interest was piqued at the sight of thick ebony hair billowing in the wind. He hit a button on the door and his window slid down in time for him to hear the sound of women's laughter floating on the air.

Maybe this trip won't be so dull after all.

Antonio rolled the limo to a stop and a second later, Quentin and Sterling rustled through the main house's eight-foot mahogany doors and into the grand foyer with its classic black-and-white marble and four angled 12-foot-tall archways.

"Hello, is anybody here?" Quentin called out.

Beatrice appeared at the top of the second-floor banister with a stack of neatly folded towels in her arms. "Mr. Quentin, Mr. Sterling, you're home."

Quentin raced up the curved staircase and wrapped his arms around the white-haired maid. "Beatrice, my love, I've finally come back to make an honest woman out of you." He planted a big, sloppy kiss against her fleshy cheek.

Beatrice's full figure quaked in his arms as she laughed at his shenanigans. "Boy, unhand me before you tempt me to really make a man out of you."

"You. Me. My bedroom at midnight. I'll provide the wine and you bring the baby oil."

She gasped. Her smooth cocoa-brown complexion flushed a deep, dark burgundy. "I, um, oh, I, um—get on now." She smacked him on the arm. "Just the devil, I swear."

Sterling just shook his head at their outrageous flirting.

Quentin laughed and released her, but when she turned and walked away, he gave her one last surprise and pinched her.

She jumped three feet and rewarded him with another smack. "Go on now before I put you over my knee."

"Promise?"

"Oh, you're impossible," she spat and stomped off.

Sterling climbed the stairs. "Why do you do that?" he asked, shaking his head in disapproval. "What if she files a sexual harassment suit?"

"Relax." Q laughed. "Beatrice knows I'm only teasing." He slapped his brother on the back as they headed down the hallway toward their old bedrooms. Quentin eyed his bed and thought about taking a quick nap, but the laughter outside penetrated his window. He strolled over and caught sight of the two women riding two chestnut Thoroughbreds.

He still couldn't make out who they were, but the one with the thick, rich ebony hair held his attention just by the graceful and expert way she rode and handled the animal.

"No need to be rude. I should go introduce myself." He jetted for the door and almost crashed into Antonio who was bringing up his luggage.

"Is there anything wrong, sir?" Antonio called after him.

"No. Everything's great." Q took the stairs two at a time, raced through the house and then escaped out the back door toward the stable. When he got closer, his run slowed to a light jog. The women's melodic laughter carved a smile onto his lips, but when he finally reached the fence, his smile melted and his eyes widened in shock.

"I don't believe it," he muttered, recognizing the face that had stalked him from the cover of *Vogue*.

Chapter 4

Alyssa loved horses and growing up on the Hinton estate meant that there were plenty around. Years ago Roger Hinton tried his hand at horse racing, mainly because that was what men of his stature did. However, it never really panned out. Bad luck coupled with bad investments caused her father's employer to lose interest in his Thoroughbred ambitions.

But the horses remained.

Throughout Alyssa's childhood, when she wasn't climbing a tree or shadowing Quentin whenever he came home, she was living and breathing everything about horses or swimming like a fish. Who knows, maybe one day when her career settled down a bit, she would invest in a stable of her own.

"Okay, I'm heading in," Tangela said. "My butt can't stand too much more of this."

Alyssa laughed. "But I thought we were going to race?"

"You win," Tangela announced, wincing and turning her horse toward the stable. "I'll see you back in your room."

"Fine. Be that way." Alyssa pretended to be miffed. "Tell Jimmie, I'm going to keep Charlie here out a little longer." She leaned forward and stroked Charlie's long neck. "You don't mind, do you, boy?"

Charlie shook his head. Alyssa smiled and patted the top of his head.

"I think he likes you," a masculine voice rang out, startling both Alyssa and Charlie.

With a quick, firm squeeze of her thighs, Alyssa kept Charlie under her control while she turned her head to see Quentin standing at the fence and smiling back at her. Alyssa sucked in a surprise gasp but in the next second a wide smile blossomed across her face. "Well, the feeling is mutual," she said, finally responding to his statement.

Q opened the fence and stepped inside. "That's good. It's good to know that the animals are in such good care."

Alyssa's gaze followed his languid strut toward her and Charlie. It sort of reminded her of one of those slick panthers she'd seen on the Discovery Channel. Plus, there was an unusual look on his face. One she recognized, but one that had never been directed toward her before: lust. Pure and simple and raw as hell.

The muscles in her stomach quivered like Jell-O while she struggled to suck enough oxygen into her lungs in order not to pass out.

"You look like a natural up there," he praised. "Been riding long?"

Her smile dimmed a little at the odd question. "Most of my life," she answered.

Quentin stopped before Charlie and reached up to stroke his head. "Hey, boy. How are you doing?"

Charlie stepped forward and nuzzled the side of Quentin's face.

"Whoa, boy. Whoa." He laughed. "You know I don't get down like that."

Alyssa laughed and with her thighs commanded Charlie to step back. "It looks like he missed you."

Q ruffled Charlie's mane. "Well, I don't make it home too often." He glanced up at her. "You here for the wedding?"

"Wouldn't have missed it for the world."

"Really? Are you a friend or family of the bride?"

Alyssa's smile vanished as she blinked at him. *He doesn't know who I am.* That knowledge, at first, dismayed her, but then slowly her mischievous side took over and her smile returned.

"No. Actually the groom invited me."

"Ah, Alfred." Q's eyes lit up. "He's a good man, you know. He's been working here a long time. He's like family to most of us."

"Yes, he speaks very fondly of the Hintons."

Quentin cocked his head. "I heard you tell your friend that you wanted to race. Still game?"

"What—you think you can beat me?"

"You're not afraid of a challenge, are you?" Excitement crept into his voice. "I don't want to toot my own horn, but I'm quite an established rider."

Alyssa snickered at the outrageous lie. Stories of Quentin's lackluster riding skills were notorious among the staff, but damn if Alyssa could stop herself from wanting to have a little fun. "All right. You're on."

Q flashed her another smile that caused her heart to race.

"Wait right here," he said. "I'll be right back."

"Yes, sir." She gave him a faux salute and then watched as he trotted off. Shifting in her saddle, Alyssa took her time to soak in his back profile. Not much had changed over the years. The philandering playboy kept himself in tip-top shape and his effect on her senses was just as strong as it had ever been. Had she really seen lust in his eyes or had she imagined the whole thing? After so many years of hoping and praying for such a miracle, she didn't quite trust her read on the situation.

Don't get your hopes up too high. As soon as he learns who you are that look in his eyes is going to quickly turn into disappointment. Alyssa weighed that information for a moment before her mischievous side spoke up. *But until he finds out, there's no reason why you can't have a little fun.*

Minutes later, Quentin emerged from the stables with Midnight, a gorgeous black stallion that was clearly a superior horse to playful Charlie, but given that Q was going to be the rider, she still liked her chances of winning a race—provided he managed to remain topside.

"Beautiful, isn't he?" Q asked, fishing for a compliment for his choice.

"He's definitely that," she admitted. "I'm almost tempted to change my mind." Quentin's beautiful smile exploded across his face, causing Alyssa's Jell-O belly to quiver once again.

"I promise I'll take it a little easy on you."

"Are you suggesting that you'll throw the race?" she asked. "That kind of defeats the purpose, doesn't it?"

"I'm just trying to be gentlemanly. Say, I give you a ten-second head start?"

Alyssa shook her head. "That's all right. I'd rather win fair and square or not at all." Quentin's laugh boomed and cloaked Alyssa like a warm blanket. She discreetly pinched her hand to make sure that she wasn't dreaming.

"You know what? I think I like you, Ms…?" He cocked his head. "I don't believe I caught your name."

"That's because I haven't given it to you yet," she answered with a teasing smile.

"Ah." Q nodded his approval. "Playing the mysterious card, eh? You know I'll find out sooner or later."

That was what she was afraid of. "I tell you what.

We'll race to the estate's entrance and back. If you win I'll tell you my name."

Quentin didn't answer. Instead he kept his gaze leveled on her. "No deal."

Alyssa's eyebrows sprang up in surprise.

"How about if I win I get a kiss?"

She blinked, her heart now forging its way up her throat. "You want to kiss someone you don't even know?"

"Scared?"

"Of you?" she asked, smiling. "Hardly."

"Then it's a deal?"

Alyssa stared. Suddenly the idea of winning didn't sound so appealing. "All right. Deal."

Quentin led Midnight toward the fence's gate and then waited patiently as Alyssa trotted behind him. Once she was out, he worked his way up into the saddle. He wasn't exactly smooth about it and Midnight seemed to sense that he didn't know what he was doing and started trotting off a bit.

"Whoa. Whoa. Come back here, boy," Quentin instructed, pulling back on the horse's reins.

Midnight ignored him and kept trotting in the opposite direction.

"No, boy. This way." Quentin pulled the reins to the right. "C'mon, Midnight. Stop playing. Let's go this way."

Alyssa snickered and quickly covered her mouth with her hand. She watched as Quentin and horse continued their battle of the wills for a few seconds before she took pity on him. She trotted Charlie over and took over Q's reins.

"C'mon, Midnight," she said gently.

The horse's ears perked and then he allowed Alyssa to lead the way.

Quentin frowned. "Oh, you're just going to play me like that?" he asked Midnight.

Midnight whinnied, but trotted alongside Charlie.

"Are you sure that you still want to do this?" Alyssa asked, fighting hard not to laugh.

"Absolutely." Q held out his hand.

She gave him back the reins and shrugged. "All right. It's your neck."

His gaze returned and lingered on her face. "It'll all be worth it in the end."

Heat rushed into Alyssa's face. "You still have to win." She leaned forward in her saddle. "Ready?"

Quentin sneaked a peek at his mysterious model's backside. Good Lord, the woman's pictures didn't do her justice. She was a walking, talking masterpiece and he was looking forward to all the games they could play during this weekend.

She glanced back at him and asked again, "Ready?"

He took a deep breath, tightened his hold on the reins and then prayed a quick prayer. "Ready, set…Go!"

Midnight and Charlie took off.

It was probably not a good idea to race with one's eyes closed, Quentin realized, but reason fled and fear took over. Midnight's powerful gallop and the fierce wind rushing against his face, quite frankly scared the bejesus out of him. What the hell was he thinking? He could be killed on this animal, he realized belatedly. Why was it that he always lost his mind when it came to competing for a beautiful woman?

Just stay in the saddle and hold on tight he coached himself. But shouldn't he at least see if he was winning? Quentin strained to peek between his eyelids. To his surprise Charlie had pulled in front of Midnight. Yet he still had a pretty good view of his competitor's lovely rump.

"Ya! Ya!" He snapped his reins in another sign of sheer lunacy. After that he wasn't quite sure what happened. All he knew was something hit him. Hard. Next thing he knew he was airborne. When he finally smacked the ground every ounce of air fled his lungs.

"Quentin!"

He heard his name but wasn't sure from which direction. How did she know his name?

"My God, are you all right?" Ms. Sexy Model asked, rushing over to him.

Quentin heard the rush of horse hooves and then a pair of feet hitting the ground.

"Quentin, please speak to me. Are you all right?"

He tried to speak. Really he did. But the act seemed as hard for him as figuring out a calculus problem. His clock had been thoroughly cleaned.

"Maybe I better go get some help?" she said.

Quentin finally managed to groan, and as a reward she gathered him into her arms. He smiled, languishing in the cheap thrill of his head being pressed against her bosom. Of course that was over with the minute she started smacking him on the face.

"Quentin, please speak to me."

When her embrace loosened, he reached out to stop her. "No. No. Don't go," he croaked.

"Oh, thank God. You're all right."

"Well, I wouldn't go that far."

"Are you in pain? Where does it hurt?"

What? Was she kidding? His entire body was in pain. "I think…I think, I'm broken."

"What? What's broken?" She leaned forward, to make sure she could hear him.

"Everything is broken," he said, convinced that it was a true statement. He should just lie there and die peacefully in her arms.

"I better go get you help." The concern in her voice thickened.

"No. I'm going to be all right. Just give me a second," he said, snuggling closer. "What happened?"

"Tree branch. You didn't duck. You ran dead into it. I don't see how you could have missed it."

He probably wouldn't have if he'd been riding with his eyes open, but he wasn't about to tell her that. Instead, Quentin groaned, pitifully. "I guess this means I lost the bet." He tried to move, but gave up when more pain shot through his body. Maybe he did need help. Midnight cantered back into view and Quentin frowned. "Demon horse. You could have killed me."

"I don't think you should be blaming Midnight," she admonished gently.

"Don't tell me you're taking his side." Quentin's gaze shifted to her. He smiled. She really did have the face of an angel. And those dark eyes…

Something tugged at him. Something in his memory. "Why do I feel like I know you?"

Her smile faded. "Do you think you could stand up?"

"Actually, I'm comfortable right where I am. It's almost as good as winning that kiss. Of course," he went on, "you could always take pity on me and kiss me anyway."

An adorable blush crept into her face.

"I was going to win anyway," he lied.

She threw her head back with a laugh. "Hardly."

"Come on," he whined. "Don't you want me to get my strength back?"

Her eyes narrowed. "What kind of trick is this? Did you hit that tree branch on purpose, since you knew you were going to *lose?*"

Quentin laughed and winced from the pain. "You're giving me way too much credit. No one takes a blow like that on purpose." He chuckled. "Unless he knew it would work." Their gazes locked again. "Is it working?"

She laughed, and he found he loved its lyrical sound. Actually he was beginning to like everything about her. "One kiss," he said, mentally willing her to say yes.

She hesitated, weighing her decision.

Was his heart racing?

"I don't know if that's such a good idea," she finally said. "There's a chance you might regret it."

"Not unless you tell me that you're my long-lost sister or something. Then that would be weird. We would probably have to move farther south."

"No. It's nothing like that."

"Then kiss me," he said.

"All right." She smiled. "But don't say I didn't warn you."

Slowly she leaned down and Quentin couldn't remember ever anticipating anything this much in his entire life. As she drew nearer, their eyes closed and their lips finally touched. It was quite possibly the sweetest kiss he had ever tasted. When he dipped his tongue inside her mouth, he couldn't believe how much she tasted like pure honey and he moaned at its sweetness. He lifted his arm and hooked it around her neck to pull her closer. How easy it would be for someone to become addicted to her. If it wasn't for his lungs screaming for oxygen, he would have never let her go.

"God. Why in the hell would I ever regret that?" he asked, panting.

She simply smiled. "We better get you up to the house." She stood and helped him up onto his feet.

He moaned and groaned the entire way.

"How do you feel?" she asked.

"After that kiss, I believe I'll live."

She blushed again, but he shook his head. "Surely, you can tell me your name now."

"Why? Because I kissed you? Hardly sounds like a reason to me."

Quentin's eyebrows spiked in amusement.

She grabbed hold of Charlie's reins and started to walk him back to the stable.

Quentin grabbed Midnight's reins and rushed after her. "So where have you been all my life?"

Her laughter danced back at him.

"C'mon. How much longer are you going to play this game? You know I'm going to find out."

"Quentin!" Sterling shouted, coming toward them. "Have you seen Alfred around?"

"No. I haven't seen him."

Sterling's gaze swung toward Q's new model-friend and a smile bloomed across his face.

Out of possessiveness, Quentin moved closer and draped an arm around her shoulder.

"Well, I'll be doggone," Sterling said. "Look who's all grown-up."

Quentin frowned and then swung his gaze between Sterling and his mysterious woman.

"Hello, Sterling," she said.

She knew Sterling's name, too?

"I've been looking all over the place for your father. Have you seen him?"

"Her father?" Q's gaze zoomed in on her. "Alfred's your father?"

She nodded.

"Then that would mean…" His eyes widened as recognition finally settled in. "Alice?"

"Alyssa," Sterling corrected.

She shrugged sheepishly. "Surprise."

Chapter 5

Alyssa waited with bated breath for Q's reaction. So far, he could do little more than bulge his eyes and sputter.

"I hear that congratulations are in order," Sterling said, also taking his full measure of Alyssa. "I hear you're a famous model nowadays. I'm sorry but I haven't had a chance to see any of your work, but I must say that from where I stand you've blossomed into a beautiful flower. Isn't that right, Q?"

"Absolutely."

Alyssa smiled graciously. "Thank you." It wasn't any surprise to her that Sterling would know little about the world of modeling and high fashion.

Sterling Hinton rarely pulled his nose away from financial spreadsheets and corporate negotiations.

"Actually, I have had the pleasure of seeing some of your work," Q admitted.

Alyssa blinked. Did that mean he knew who she was all along?

"You're on this month's cover of *Vogue,* am I right?"

"That's right." Her smile broadened with pleasure.

"Of course I didn't match your beautiful face with the memory of my little Alice," he added. "I feel like a fool now."

His Alice?

"Shame on you for holding out on me," he said, with a teasing smile. "It wasn't very nice of you to take advantage of me like that."

His Alice?

"It wasn't quite like that," she reminded him while trying to ignore the quivering of her belly and how her knees weakened beneath the power of his dimples. "I did tell you that you would regret it."

"In that case…you were wrong."

Their gazes met and held for a long moment. The afternoon's breeze cooled Alyssa's heated face as the memory of their kiss replayed in her head.

"Humph!" Sterling cleared his throat. Alyssa jumped. She'd forgotten that he was still standing there. She flashed him an embarrassed smile.

"Well, congratulations again," Sterling said. "Maybe I'll see if Alfred is in the east wing." He turned toward Quentin. "Maybe you should come with me?"

"Um, actually—"

"Great!" Sterling made it clear that he wouldn't take no for an answer. "Between the two of us, we will be able to find him in no time."

Quentin drew a deep breath, but gave in to his brother's silent pressure. "Of course. Though I can't imagine what could be so urgent."

Sterling ignored the comment and fluttered another smile at Alyssa. "Will we see you tonight at dinner?"

"Absolutely." She glanced at Quentin. "Don't worry," she said. "I can take Midnight to the stable for you." She took hold of the reins. "I think he likes me better anyway."

"That makes two of us." He winked.

"All righty." Sterling tossed his arm around Quentin's shoulders. "Come on, bro. No need to make a nuisance out of yourself."

From the look on his face, Q was obviously annoyed, but he offered no resistance as Sterling pulled him away from Alyssa's side.

Alyssa watched the brothers stroll away, while a knowing smile remained plastered across her face. *His Alice.*

Once she hated that he never seemed to remember her name—but now *Alice* held new meaning for her. It felt more like a lover's pet name—something intimate…and possessive.

Hadn't he always been her Quentin?

Her Q?

Alyssa turned toward the stables feeling both

giddy and mischievous. Was this actually happening? Was there a chance for her to win the heart of her childhood crush? An undeniable wave of hope blossomed, while an old fantasy of becoming Mrs. Quentin Dwayne Hinton started to feel more like a real possibility.

After returning both Charlie and Midnight to the stables, Alyssa practically floated back to the servants' quarters and to her old bedroom. She found Tangela sprawled across the floral and lace bedding with her head buried beneath the pillows.

"Don't tell me it's time to get up," Tangela said, her voice muffled because she refused to remove the pillows. "My whole backside is killing me. Just let me lie here for a couple of years."

Alyssa sighed as she closed the door and then floated her way over to the bed. "Don't worry. Take all the time you need." She sighed again.

When Tangela didn't pick up on her mood, Alyssa gave a deeper—longer sigh.

Tangela grunted, and finally lifted the pillow from her head. "All right. All right. I'll bite. What happened?"

"Quentin is home."

Tangela's head popped up, her face awash with curiosity. "And?"

"And…" Alyssa turned giggly. "He kissed me."

"Shut up!" Tangela's jaw dropped open. Her eyes doubled in size.

"I know. Can you believe it?"

"Shut up!" Tangela sprang up onto her knees and

stared down at her best friend. "You're lying. You gotta be lying."

"Nope." Alyssa jumped off the bed and launched into a victory dance. "It was unbelievable! Magical!"

Tangela, now with a surge of energy, leaped from the bed and danced with Alyssa. As far back as elementary school, Alyssa had shared her dreams of marrying Q with her best friend. Tangela knew every embarrassing story of Alyssa following Quentin around like a puppy.

"But wait," Tangela said, stopping in midgroove. "I thought you said that you were over Quentin?"

Alyssa shrugged, sheepishly. "I lied."

"Did you see the curves on that girl?" Quentin asked his brother as they strolled into their father's library. "Little Alice Jansen."

"Her name is Alyssa," Sterling said, his face growing more sour by the second. "And *you* stay away from her."

Quentin's thumb stabbed his chest. "Me? What did I do?"

Sterling finally pivoted around to level his younger brother with a sharp gaze. "That's the question I should be asking you. What were you two doing out there?"

"Nothing," Q protested with mock innocence.

Sterling rolled his eyes. "Want to try that look with someone that doesn't know you like the back of their hand? You're the last person on earth to be trusted with a beautiful woman."

"Aha! So at least you admit she's beautiful?"

"Of course I admit it. I'm not blind. But that's hardly the point."

Q laughed and strolled over to the minibar in the corner of the library. "Then what's the point, bro?"

"And she's Alfred's daughter! She's not some plaything you can toy with and then cast aside the moment you get bored. Good God, the girl is practically part of the family."

Q laughed. "No blood of mine runs through her veins, which makes her fair game."

"Fair game?" Sterling thundered, storming up behind him. "Listen to you. You should be ashamed of yourself for even considering hitting on that girl. She spent most of her childhood ogling you."

Quentin frowned. "How old do you think she is now?"

"It doesn't matter. Stay away from her."

Q glanced at his brother, surprised at his level of anger. "Oh c'mon, Sterling. In case you haven't noticed, Alice is a grown woman now."

"Alyssa."

"And she is quite capable of making decisions for herself. We both are. We don't need you or anybody else to play chaperone."

"We? What's this we stuff? And what about Alfred? How do you think he would feel about you pursuing his daughter?"

Quentin paused, his confident smile dimmed. "Alfred and I have always gotten along."

"That's not what I asked you," Sterling said. "Alfred, like anyone else in this house, knows your reputation. And he, like the rest of us, knows about Alyssa's crush on you. Do you *really* think he'll be happy if you pursued her?"

Quentin finished making his drink and took a deep gulp. "There's no need to make me feel like a child molester."

"Then stop behaving like one."

The brothers fell silent for a long moment, while Q looked as if he was truly thinking the situation over. The problem was that he'd already kissed Alyssa, and he was having a hard time trying to erase the taste of her lips from his mouth. The alcohol sure in hell wasn't doing the job. Hell, he could still smell the sweet scent of her perfume.

And those curves…

Heaven help him.

"Quentin," Sterling said with an unmistakable, commanding tone. "For once in your life, do the right thing."

Q took another long gulp from his drink before he finally settled on a response. "I'll think about it."

Chapter 6

The last thing Sterling wanted or had time to do was play babysitter to his younger brother. But given this latest development, or rather the way Alyssa Jansen had developed, he had no choice but to do just that. That raw unadulterated lust he just witnessed in his brother's eyes meant one thing: trouble.

Quentin had never been a man who listened to reason, especially when a beautiful woman was involved. Sterling drew in several deep breaths, trying to calm his anger and anxiety, but the exercise was futile at best. Entering the kitchen, Sterling hoped to grab something light to eat since it was still hours away from dinner.

"Oh, Alfred, there you are," he said, noticing the

large man hunched over the counter and poring over some paperwork. "I was looking for you earlier."

Alfred glanced up with a casual smile. "You know, I'm never too far from the kitchen." He chuckled.

Sterling grabbed an apple from a crystal bowl in the center of one of the marble countertops. "Not for much longer, though, right?"

Alfred chuckled. "Right."

"It'll be strange around here once you're gone. I'm surprised my father hasn't offered to double your salary to get you to stay."

"Oh, he has."

"And you turned him down?"

"Yep. And then he tripled it."

Sterling whistled. "When Dad wants something, he doesn't usually take no for an answer."

"There's a first time for everything," Alfred said. "Just like there's a time for a man to move on—to start living out some of his own dreams."

Sterling's eyebrows climbed at the melancholy tenor of Alfred's voice. He had known the large, lovable lion for a long time. He took great honor in calling him a friend. Frankly speaking, the man was hands down one of the best chefs he'd ever known. "Care to share some of those dreams you have in mind?"

Alfred's gaze found his, as if weighing whether Sterling was truly interested or not. "Well," he began. "I figured I'd strike out and make a name for myself as a celebrity chef. I'm waiting to hear back about a possible television show. Estelle even thinks I could put a proposal together for my own cookbook."

Impressed, Sterling beamed at him. "Then I'll know two famous Jansens."

Alfred's chest puffed up. "You heard about Alyssa then?"

"Beatrice may have mentioned it a time or two. I'm sure you're proud."

"Only because she's happy. That's all a parent really wants." Alfred drew a deep breath. His gaze shifted onto nothing in particular. "I think Melissa would have been proud."

The silence that trailed his proclamation made Sterling uneasy. Alfred had rarely talked about his deceased wife. Sterling couldn't remember if he had ever known the story about how Alfred became a widower. Jeez. How was it that he knew so little about a man he considered a good friend? Hadn't he just told Q that Alfred and his daughter were practically family?

"Anyway," Alfred said, coming out of his daydream. "Alyssa is my pride and joy, and I would've been happy no matter what she decided to do. Now it's my turn. I just hope she and Estelle hit it off."

"They haven't met?"

"Yes and no." He sucked in a deep breath. "They'll meet tonight for the first time in a while. I'll be honest. I'm a little nervous."

Sterling smiled. "It's going to be all right. I'm sure Alyssa also wants you to be happy."

"Yeah," Alfred said thoughtfully. "I just don't want her to think I'm trying to replace her mother. No one could ever do that…but sometimes a man gets tired of being lonely." Their eyes locked. Alfred looked as if he was surprised he'd said the words out loud.

Sterling was a bit surprised himself, but his words also made an unmistakable connection.

"I don't know," Alfred said, as he immediately backtracked. "Ever since Alyssa left and started traveling the world, it's just been me and my work here—not that I'm complaining," he added. "But…it's just time. You know?"

Sterling nodded his head and turned his gaze away from his friend. He, unlike his brothers, was more married to his work than not. The few relationships he'd drifted into never lasted long because he was always willing to work the long hours and fly from one job site to another at the drop of a dime. He'd unintentionally stood up more women than he cared to count. But one day…

"Well, you found someone to share the next phase of your life with," Sterling said. "That's a step in the right direction." As if he would know, but it at least sounded good.

Alfred nodded. "Right." He stood, but almost immediately doubled over.

Sterling dropped his apple and raced around the corner to grab Alfred by the shoulders. "Hey, hey. Are you all right?"

Alfred caught and steadied himself against the

counter. "Yeah. I guess I just got a little woozy there for a second." He laughed awkwardly.

Sterling frowned, not sure what to make of what he had just witnessed. "Are you sure? Maybe you should sit back down." He turned and reached for the stool that had clacked to the floor.

"No. No. I'm all right." Alfred adjusted his tall frame.

Sterling dropped his arms and stepped back. It was clear he didn't want his help.

"I've been running around so much I hadn't bothered to check my blood sugar," Alfred said with a chuckle. "I better grab a piece of fruit myself before Estelle gets on me."

Sterling nodded along. The explanation sounded stilted and forced. Alfred moved toward the fruit bowl. "No need to upset her," he added.

Sterling caught the hint. "Mum's the word."

Alfred nodded and took a healthy bite out of the apple. In the next second, he made a hasty retreat from the kitchen, leaving Sterling to mull over what had just happened.

Sterling picked his apple up from the floor and tossed it into the garbage. "It's none of my business," he mumbled under his breath. Just how many people did he want to add to his babysitting duties anyway?

He returned to the fruit bowl; this time, he grabbed a banana and then strolled out of the kitchen. By the time he hit the first step on the staircase, the front door opened and he turned to see his older brother, Jonas, and his wife, Toni, enter the house.

"Uncle Sterling!" Little Kerry shot past her parents and launched toward him.

Before he had time to react, Kerry's small arms wrapped around his legs and threatened to tip him over all the stairs. "Whoa. Well, look who I have here," Sterling boasted, leaning over to give his niece a hug. "Let me take a good look at you."

Kerry released her death grip and stood back so she could perform a perfect pirouette to show off her beautiful orange dress. "Do you like it?" she asked eagerly. "Mommy helped me pick it out."

"Is that right?" Sterling glanced up at a beaming Toni and then back down at his niece. "I think you look beautiful."

"Thank you," she said, curtsying and lacing her fingers into his. "Do you know where Uncle Quentin is? Daddy said he was going to be here."

"He's around here someplace. He's probably upstairs in his room."

"Yea!" Kerry released Sterling's hand and then shot up the stairs.

"Ouch. That hurts." Sterling laughed.

"Don't take it personal, bro," Jonas said, lugging in more bags. "Q always had a way with the ladies—of all ages."

Sterling moved toward the door to offer a helping hand, but was briefly delayed with a brotherly hug, followed by an awkward embrace with his sister-in-law, who still held his sleeping nephew. "Looks like he is knocked out."

She laughed. "I wish he would've slept during the flight, too. Instead he raised so much hell, I wouldn't be surprised if the airline banned us for life."

"You could've taken the jet," Sterling reminded them.

Toni rolled her eyes. "Wasteful spending," she muttered. "I swear the money you boys waste on your frivolous toys." She shook her head as she strolled toward the staircase.

"Why do you always go there with her?" Jonas asked, laughing. "You should have heard her when Antonio picked us up at the airport in the limo. Mark my words, she'll have Dad investing in hybrids by the time we leave here."

Sterling laughed and grabbed a few bags.

"Then she'll definitely have her work cut out for her," he said, climbing up the stairs behind his older brother.

"Don't underestimate her. She's on this whole environmental kick now. Our entire house is under major construction to be more eco-friendly. Solar panels, wind turbines—consider yourself warned," Jonas said, entering their usual guest room.

"Consider himself warned about what?" Toni asked. She placed little Denzel in bed.

"Nothing," Jonas lied, but he looked as though he had just got caught with his hand inside the cookie jar.

Toni's eyes narrowed, but a smile curved the

corners of her lips. "How many times have I told you you're a horrible liar?"

"Too many times to count." Jonas rolled his eyes as he slipped a loving arm around Toni's waist.

"Uh-huh." She peppered his cheek with kisses. "So what were you two talking about?"

"Nothing much. We were just talking about Sterling's…love life," Jonas tried lying again.

This time Toni took the bait. "Really?"

Sterling frowned, wondering why his brother was so determined to hang him out to dry.

"Are you seeing someone?" Toni asked. Her eyes shone.

Sterling didn't like being put on the spot. "No—not exactly," he said. "You know me—work, work, work."

Disappointment pinched Toni's face. "We're going to have to do something about that. You're a great guy and…"

"I'm sure you will make some lucky woman a great husband," said Sterling and Jonas, finishing her sentence for her.

"That really is a horrible thing to say to someone, honey," Jonas said.

Toni crossed her arms and narrowed her gaze between the two brothers. "Fine. Just forget I said anything."

Sterling was happy to do just that when she pointed a finger at him. "But you're not getting any younger, and all the money in the world can't replace the love of a good woman. It's not the end of the world to settle down and start a family. Isn't that right, honey?" Toni slid into Jonas's arms.

"Right, baby."

The smile that spread across Jonas's face stirred Sterling's jealousy. "I'm getting out of here. You two are nauseating."

"Oh, Sterling, come back," Toni called after him, but he was determined to make his escape while he still had the chance.

"Baby, let him go. He's a big boy. He'll know when it's time for him to settle down." Jonas laughed. "It'll be right about the time he goes insane."

Chapter 7

Alyssa couldn't believe how nervous she was to actually be meeting her father's girlfriend. Not girl-friend but fiancée and future stepmother. The title was a hard one to get used to. Throughout her life, she couldn't remember a single time when her father showed any interest in a woman. If he'd ever dated after her mother's death, he certainly kept it from her. But what if she didn't like this woman? What if she was some evil, wicked stepmother with two horrible daughters like in "Cinderella"?

Alyssa perked up.

Did Estelle have children of her own? She had no clue and it hadn't occurred to her to ask her father. She suddenly felt uneasy with the idea of sharing her father's affection—not just with another woman but possibly with a whole other family. Even as the thought drifted across her mind, she realized that she was being selfish. Still, there was a part of her that couldn't help it. She had become so accustomed to being Daddy's little girl that she didn't know how to be any other way.

"What are you thinking so hard about?" Tangela asked, glancing up from her *Essence* magazine.

"Nothing." Alyssa shrugged, but she was unable to remove the frown from her face.

"It doesn't look like nothing to me."

Alyssa sighed. What was the point of lying to her best friend? The beauty of having known someone for so long was the ability to share everything with them without fear of being judged. "I'm just trying to get used to the idea of having a stepmom." Alyssa finished hanging her clothes in the closet. "I don't know what to expect."

Tangela shook her head and rolled her eyes. "Trust me. It's no big deal. My father is on his fourth marriage and my mom is on her third. After a while you just get used to a revolving door of new faces." With a shrug, Tangela turned her attention back to her magazine.

Alyssa frowned at Tangela's cynical point of view. Once upon a time, Tangie had stressed over her parents' latest marriages or new children. It was probably why Tangie rarely went home anymore. It was sad to see the close bond she once shared with her parents erode over time.

Was that what was in store for her and her father? What if her father and Estelle started having children of their own? That was still possible, right?

"I think I'm going to be sick."

A knock rattled her door.

"Come in," Alyssa called out.

The door opened and her father poked his head inside of the room. When his gaze found Alyssa near the closet, his lips stretched across his face. "I have someone here I want you to meet...again."

Alyssa shot a look at her best friend. This was it: The moment of truth.

Tangela stood up from the bed while Alyssa tried to match her father's exuberance with a bright smile of her own.

"Great. Bring her in," she said.

Her father widened the door and stepped into the small bedroom with a smiling, elegant woman hanging on to his arm. It had been years since Alyssa had been in Estelle's elementary class but the moment their gazes locked, Alyssa felt seven years old and consumed with the desire to please.

"Estelle, this is my baby girl, Alyssa. Alyssa, this is Estelle."

"Hello," the women chimed in unison.

Estelle sputtered, "I'm so glad that you were able to make it to the wedding this weekend. I mean with it being such short notice and all," she laughed.

"Well, it did sound like a shotgun sort of thing," Alyssa laughed, taking advantage of the opening.

To her amazement, her father's face darkened. Her antennae sprang up. "You're not…you two aren't…"

Estelle glanced nervously at her father.

"Actually, I was going to talk to you about that." He looked over at Tangela.

"You know what," Tangie said, picking up on the hint. "I'm just going to run out to the…um…someplace." She rushed over to Alyssa, squeezed her hand for moral support and then darted around Alfred and Estelle and then out the door.

Now that it was just the three of them, it seemed as though the oxygen was trying to escape the room.

"Maybe I should sit down." Light-headed, Alyssa walked over to the bed and perched herself on the edge. "A baby," she mumbled. The word and the concept seemed foreign.

"Now, Ally. I know that this is a big surprise to you," her father said, sitting down next to her.

"You think?"

Alfred took her hand into his and laced their fingers together. "I'd hoped that you'd be happy for us."

Guilt crashed against Alyssa's heart, causing her to be ashamed of her selfishness. She drew a deep breath and glanced up. "Of course I'm happy for you," she said, her gaze fluttering to Estelle. "For *both* of you. I just—I just need to get used to the fact that—I'm going to be an older sister," she boasted, though a lump still swelled in her throat, choking her.

Her father beamed as he released her hand and then crushed her against his chest. "Oh, baby girl. I knew that you'd be happy for us."

Tears burned at the back of her eyes as she soaked in her father's affection. "Yes, Dad. I'm really happy for you."

Roger and Kitty Hinton surprised Alfred and Estelle and their small wedding party by treating them to the exclusive five-star Magnolia's restaurant. The entire Hinton staff and their spouses were in attendance, and quite frankly it was a shock to Alyssa to see Beatrice down a whole bottle of Dom Pérignon by herself. On the opposite end, the more Antonio drank the more Italian he spoke.

Kitty spent most of the time slipping Billy Dee Williams the third, her much-beloved and bejeweled Chihuahua, pieces of filet mignon and cooing, "Aw. That's a good mama's baby."

Alyssa shook her head at the way the woman continued to baby that dog.

The food was rich and bountiful. The laughs were loud and contagious, but most of all, Alfred and Estelle were happy. Wasn't that all that mattered?

Forever on a diet, Alyssa and Tangie picked over their food and instead just indulged in how wonderful everything smelled.

To Alyssa's surprise, Sterling made an effort to include Tangie in conversation. "So what is it that you do, Ms. Graham? I seem to remember you and

Alyssa being quite the dynamic duo when you were younger. Like the time when you two had a giant bubble bath in the Jacuzzi."

Alyssa and Tangie glanced at each other and giggled at the memory.

"You remember that?" Tangie asked.

"It's kind of hard not to remember half the back lawn overflowing with strawberry bubble bath," he chuckled.

"It was Alyssa's idea," Tangie confessed, pointing at her best friend. "*She* poured the whole bottle in there."

Alyssa gasped. "Judas!"

They laughed. When they'd calmed down, Tangie answered Sterling's question. "Well, actually, we're still a dynamic duo. I'm Ally's assistant."

"A wonderful assistant at that," Alyssa said, pumping up her friend. "She keeps my head and my schedule straight. I would be completely lost without her."

"Oh, is that right?" Sterling said, nodding. "Have you thought about modeling yourself?"

The question clearly surprised Tangie. She had long thought that the extra weight on her short frame disqualified her in the modeling profession. Alyssa lost count how many times she'd tried to open Tangie's eyes to her own beauty, only to have her friend find fault with everything from her slight double chin to her thick thighs.

Sterling's innocence and sincerity would no doubt

do wonders for Tangie's self-esteem, and Alyssa was grateful to him for that. Of course, Sterling had always had such a kind heart, though he usually buried himself in work so very few people got a chance to see it.

She watched him out of the corners of her eyes for a few seconds.

"You sure are quiet," Quentin said. His warm breath rushed against her ear and sent a delicious thrill through her.

"I'm just enjoying the evening," she answered, taking a quick glance over her shoulder. "What about you?"

Quentin eased in close. "I'm enjoying myself *now* and, of course when I won that kiss this afternoon."

"You *didn't* win," she reminded him.

"You have your version and I have mine. Either way, I walked away with a kiss."

"I felt sorry for you."

"Then maybe I should fall down more often."

Alyssa chuckled and shook her head. "You know you would have never won that race. Everyone knows you're a lousy rider."

"Aha! So you were setting me up to fail. You never intended for me to win my prize." He cocked his head. "Unless you were going to throw the race."

Her face darkened with guilt.

"Ah." The corners of Q's lips quirked up. "Not only has little Alice grown up, but she's learned how to play the games women play. Tsk. Tsk. Tsk." He shook his head, but his eyes remained mischievous. "How disappointing."

Alyssa lifted a delicate brow. "And what about the game *you* were playing?" she challenged. "You really could have broken your neck riding like that."

Q's smile remained playful. "Maybe." He leaned in close. His seductive and heady cologne engulfed her. "But frankly, I think it was well worth it. Who knows, maybe we can do it again?"

Speech eluded Alyssa as Quentin's bedroom eyes dragged her under a spell. She reached for her wine-glass in hopes of dousing the flames now licking the insides of her belly, but one sip of her drink only caused them to roar more out of control.

"So tell us, Alyssa," Mrs. Hinton nearly shouted from across the raucous table. "Have you given much thought to going from modeling to acting? Lord knows you have the face for it."

"You certainly do," Quentin whispered.

His praise only caused her blush to deepen. "I, um, haven't really given it any thought," she answered shyly.

"Well, if you ask me," Mrs. Hinton continued, "you'd be a natural. Now back when *I* was on Broadway, stars were really stars. They had mystery and class." She leaned toward her husband. "Isn't that right, honey?"

"That's right, pumpkin." Roger lifted her hand and placed a kiss against her wedding ring.

Turning her broad smile back toward Alyssa, Mrs.

Hinton's eyes glossed over. "It was truly like being a part of American royalty."

Alyssa bit her lower lip and judging by a few amused gazes, she realized that Mrs. Hinton was just getting warmed up for her stroll down memory lane, retelling stories her family had all heard a million times. From her heyday as an understudy in August Wilson's *Fences* to how Isaac from *The Love Boat* made a pass at her in front of her husband. Of course Mrs. Hinton's rendition never included the absolutely horrid reviews she received for her performances, but the family, as well as the staff, just exchanged knowing looks.

The minute there was a pause in the conversation, Alfred jumped in. "Well, I have an announcement to make."

Alyssa blinked and then inched down in her seat. Was he about to announce the pregnancy to the whole group? Her stomach muscles looped into tight knots as everyone gave Alfred their undivided attention.

Her father smiled and looped his large arm around Estelle's shoulder. "I received a call this afternoon about a job in Atlanta."

A job? Alyssa frowned.

"I thought you were just retiring," Roger cut in, looking put off. "If you wanted a new job—"

"This is more than *just* a job—it's an opportunity," he said, still smiling.

It was clear by Roger's expression that he didn't like the sound of that. He was a very competitive man and the idea of someone luring his favorite chef from his employ was infusing red heat into his cocoa complexion.

"I'm going to have my own cooking show," Alfred announced.

Alyssa gasped in surprise while the rest of the table exploded with applause. "Daddy, are you for real?" she asked, jumping to her feet.

He bobbed his head as his eyes shone with unmistakable pride.

"Oh, I'm so thrilled for you," she said, rushing around the long rectangular table so she could wrap her arms around his broad shoulders.

"Well, well. That's quite a different story," Roger Hinton said, beaming across the table. "*That* deserves another toast."

"Hold on." Quentin stood and brought Alyssa her wine.

She remained locked in her father's arms while she accepted the offered glass. Their eyes met with a smoldering heat. A second later, her father's arms tightened against her waist.

"To the Jansens," Roger saluted. "May your good fortune continue to reign."

"Here! Here!" everyone chorused.

"And while your stars continue to rise, I hope you don't forget about your friends," Quentin added and the group chuckled.

Though his words were simple enough, there

was a wild fluttering in her center that caught his double meaning.

"Amen," Beatrice shouted.

She had him, she realized, right in the palm of her hand.

Chapter 8

"Isn't Sterling absolutely dreamy?" Tangie said the moment she and Alyssa returned to her small bedroom.

The question elicited a reflexive laugh from Alyssa. *Sterling? Dreamy?*

"He is," Tangela insisted. "He's handsome, studious, nice…and rich as hell."

"I guess. It's just…"

"It's just what?"

"I don't know." She shrugged. "He always just seems so stiff and so serious about everything," she said, even though she knew that wasn't quite true.

"Whatever. You're incapable of noticing anyone else whenever Quentin is around."

Alyssa smiled at the obvious truth. Tonight she

had practically clocked Q's every move in the restaurant, even when she was pretending not to. By the end of the night, Quentin had flirted with practically every woman in attendance, whether they were married or not. It was part of his charm. No one took him seriously.

So why did she? What made her think that he was *really* interested in her?

"Hello. Earth to Alyssa."

Tangie waved her hand in front of Alyssa's face. She jumped. "What?"

Her best friend laughed and shook her head. "Girl, you really got it bad. We've traveled all around the world and you have given every gorgeous, rich and not-so-rich bachelor one excuse after another. The minute we arrive back here, you've been behaving like a lovesick teenager. Snap out of it!"

Alyssa wished she could, but nothing on earth was going to get her to forget about that kiss—that wonderful, warm, earth-shattering kiss. She sighed and plopped down on the bed. "I just don't know if I can," she finally admitted. "I mean…what if this was really meant to be?" she asked, pulling off her shoes. "I used to sit up in this room day after day plotting and planning how to become Mrs. Quentin Dwayne Hinton. When I left for college, I thought I'd grown out of it. But now…" She glanced around. "Something about being here…and seeing him just brings all those emotions back."

"All right." Tangela sighed and then sat next to her. "So what are you going to do about it?"

"That is the big question." Alyssa stood and walked over to her bedroom window. The Hinton estate had always reminded her of some grand fairy-tale palace. Her prince was always so close and yet so far away.

"Well, if you want my opinion," Tangie said. "I say go for it. Hell, what do you have to lose? You both are adults now. Right? This is the twenty-first century. There's no rule saying that the servant's daughter can't marry up."

"Marry!" Alyssa's smile returned.

"I can't believe it. You're actually afraid of going for it." Tangie laughed. "I've never known you to be afraid of anything."

Was she afraid?

"Plus, judging by the way Quentin couldn't keep his eyes off you, I'd say you have more than a fair chance of finally snagging him with a sharp hook."

Alyssa's hopes soared, but she tried not to let it show. "C'mon. He was flirting with everyone. Even Estelle got a few winks from him."

"He was playing with them. He was *flirting* with you."

It did seem that way, she reasoned. Alyssa closed her eyes and easily recalled the press of his lips against hers. There was something wicked about the way his tongue had slid in between her lips.

Shaking her head, she erased the image. "You

know what? I think I'm going out for a swim. I need to clear my head."

"You're kidding. It's late."

"So?"

"No. I'm not wrecking my perm. If you're going, then you're going by yourself."

"Oh, c'mon. The exercise will help you sleep like a baby."

"I'm already going to sleep like a baby."

"Just for a couple of laps?"

"No. Besides, we have a full day with the wedding and all."

"Well, I'm going. I think I packed one of those swimsuits from the *SI* shoot."

"Whatever. You do you."

Twenty minutes later, Alyssa made the perfect forward dive into the Hintons' twenty-foot pool. The minute she hit the water, she felt as if she was in her element. An all-around athlete in high school, Alyssa had a wall full of trophies she'd won during her time on the swim team. For her, there was absolutely nothing better than swimming by moonlight. There was something about the total body workout that had a way of clearing her mind and working off the day's stress.

All she could think about as she made her laps around the pool was that kiss. That wonderful, glorious kiss by a man who had monopolized her dreams for as long as she could remember.

Go for it!

There was such a strong part of her that wanted to do just that, but there was that other part that reminded her of just how fast Quentin went through women. Was Quentin even capable of more than a fleeting affair?

Out of frustration she dived deeper into the pool and swam along the bottom while she mulled over the situation. Could she just accept a small part of him—or could she really go for happily ever after?

Alyssa kicked toward the surface. When she broke through, she sucked in the much-needed air. However, she immediately sensed that she was not alone. She turned toward the diving board where Quentin stood smiling back.

"Looks like you're having fun. Mind if I join you?"

Almost immediately Alyssa's heart hammered on her rib cage. Its quick pounding echoed in her ears. "It's your pool. You're free to do what you like."

Quentin pulled open his white robe and revealed a pair of black-and-white swim briefs.

Alyssa's gaze greedily drank in his impressive body: broad shoulders, narrow waist and lean, but muscular legs. The kicker was his impressive abs. She itched to run her fingers along their rippled contours.

"Do I pass inspection?"

She didn't dare answer but quietly treaded water in the center of the pool.

Quentin stepped onto the diving board and showed off by displaying a perfect arm stand and then dived into the pool.

Alyssa smiled as she watched him glide along the bottom of the pool toward her.

Being the little devil that he was, Q grabbed Alyssa's foot and tugged her under the water. He didn't hold on to her, but instead allowed her to buoy back to the top.

"Not fair," she complained, laughing.

"C'mon. You should know by now that I don't like playing fair," he said, invading her space.

"Oh yeah. It's coming back to me now." She dived under the water, giving him a brief glance of her firm, round tush.

"My, my, my."

Alyssa rocketed away, striving to place a little distance between them so she could think better.

However, Quentin meant what he said about not playing fair and charged after her. When she finally broke the surface again, he was right there. "You're a good swimmer," he said. "Your long fluid strokes are quite…graceful."

She wanted to thank him, but he'd once again locked her into his dark, probing stare. Words evaporated in her head.

"My little Alice," he said softly. His gaze effortlessly caressed her face. "I always knew that you would grow up to be a heartbreaker."

"I'm hardly that."

"No?" He lowered his voice so that she moved closer. "You mean to tell me that there's no man out there right now drowning his sorrows in the bottom of a whiskey bottle? No man trying to thaw out from your cold…shoulder?"

To her surprise, he leaned down and placed a soft kiss against her right shoulder.

"There's no man sitting by the phone waiting for you to call?" He kissed her other shoulder.

Their eyes locked again and Alyssa's chest burned from lack of oxygen. Instead of answering, she slowly shook her head.

Quentin cocked his head. "Now why don't I believe that?" His wicked smile enticed her.

Self-preservation kicked in and Alyssa leaned back and floated away. "You're pretty good," she said.

He laughed. His deep baritone rumbled across the water as he followed his prey.

"If I didn't know any better, Alice. I'd say that you were scared of me."

She stopped and treaded water in the pool. "I'm not scared of you."

Quentin's mischievous grin only spread wider. "Liar."

"Why should I be scared?" she challenged.

"Oh, I don't know." He shrugged, but there was nothing careless about it. "Maybe because that kiss we shared frightened you."

She forced out a laugh that sounded a little off, even to her. "My, what a big ego you have, Mr. Hinton."

Quentin's arm snaked out around her waist and pulled her closer before she knew what was happening. "It's 'my, what a big ego you have, *Quen-*

tin.' I certainly think we're beyond formalities. Don't you?"

Alyssa's breathing turned choppy. If it wasn't for him holding her, she was sure that she would have sunk like a stone, since her motor skills suddenly malfunctioned.

"You're trembling," he whispered.

"I'm cold."

"But it's a heated pool," he reminded her.

She shivered some more. "Why are you playing games?"

"Because I like to win." He brushed his lips against hers. Gently. "Besides, you intrigue me." His gaze lowered to her lips. "Fascinate me. Plus, if I don't kiss you again, I swear I'm going to go crazy."

Alyssa held still, neither encouraging nor discouraging his next move. And just like in her childhood fantasies, she watched mesmerized as Quentin's head descended.

What the playful couple didn't realize or even consider was their growing audience. None of them pleased at what they were witnessing.

Chapter 9

It had been years since the Hintons had hosted a wedding. And this one, like the last, was equally breathtaking. The late-fall weather was more than accommodating. The orchestra was in full swing in the temporary pavilion while guests and family trickled inside. Estelle masterfully embraced the colors of autumn. The flowers and decorations had hints of gold, rust and emerald-green. Her wedding dress was a sophisticated off-white skirt suit. The bridesmaids were arrayed in gold and burgundy. Only Alyssa wore an emerald-green number with thin spaghetti straps.

"I know this is last-minute, but I hoped you would agree to be my maid of honor."

Touched, Alyssa brushed her fingers against the soft silk and felt tears burn the backs of her eyes. "I don't know what to say," she said honestly.

"Say yes," Estelle urged. "Because I don't know anyone else here that can wear this dress."

"Of course I'll be your maid of honor. It would be a privilege."

Estelle opened her arms and Alyssa slid in for a hug. Everything was happening so fast, she could barely wrap her brain around it. Her two-member family would soon be four. There was an emotion tugging at her heart that she was afraid to name. Guilt?

Alyssa's thoughts turned to her mother.

Alyssa grew up always believing that her mother was watching over her. Her own personal guardian angel. She often pretended that her diary entries were life letters to her mother. In the last two days, she wondered whether her mother would be happy or hurt about their moving on.

Surely, she would understand.

Melissa Jansen was a face Alyssa only knew in pictures now. She was four years old when she and her mother were involved in that fatal car crash so many years ago. The doctors and police had all said that it had been a miracle that Alyssa had survived the incident with just minor scratches.

Her mother wasn't so lucky.

Alyssa pulled out of Estelle's arms and smiled kindly. "I better go try this on."

Estelle nodded in understanding and then returned to her chair where her hairdresser waited patiently.

Miraculously, Alyssa escaped the room before her tears embarrassed her. She was happy for her father, she tried to remind herself. *Happy. Happy. Happy.*

Before she reached her room, she saw her father lumbering down the hall. Their eyes caught and they shared a brief butterfly smile. He looked stunningly handsome. His long lion mane of hair was tamed while his black tux only seemed to magnify his mountainous shoulders and tall frame.

"Hey, baby girl. I see you got your dress."

Alyssa glanced down at it and nodded. "Yes. It's very beautiful. Thanks for having her ask me."

"No. It was completely her idea," he insisted, walking up to her. "She's really hoping that you two will hit it off." He cleared his throat. "I am, too."

Alyssa smiled and pretended to dust away lint from his arm. "I think she's lovely, Daddy. I'm sure you two are going to be happy." She had meant the words of encouragement, but there was a sudden sadness that paralyzed his smile. "Mom would want you to be happy, too," she said. "It's way past time."

Alfred took her hand and gave it a squeeze. "Did I ever tell you why I decided to work for Mr. Hinton in the first place?"

She shook her head.

"I thought it was the perfect place to work and raise you. You had access to the best that life had to offer. The best schools, horses—fine art. Now look at you. It was sort of perfect, really. If I'd pursued working at some fancy restaurant it would have been long hours away from you and we probably wouldn't have been so close. This way, I was able to keep my eye on you. Now you're all grown-up." He lovingly swept her hair back from her shoulders. "So beautiful. You look so much like your mother."

"Thanks, Dad."

"It was also easy to protect you here. Now you don't need my protection anymore."

"I wouldn't go that far." She elbowed him. "A girl will always need her dad around."

Alfred's eyes misted and it looked like he was struggling with his next words. "Quentin…"

She stiffened.

He seemed to pick up her resistance and backed down. "Just be careful, baby. I don't want to see you get hurt." He leaned forward and kissed the top of her head. "Thanks for being the best daughter a father could ever ask for."

It was an hour before the wedding and Sterling was already hovering above the punch bowl.

"It's usually your brother Quentin that I worry about indulging too much at one of these functions," Roger said, stepping up behind his son.

Sterling glanced over his shoulder. "Don't worry. I know my limit."

His father nodded and then reached to fill his own glass. "I have a question for you," he said.

"Shoot." Sterling turned up his drink.

"What do you know about your brother and Alfred's daughter?"

Sterling groaned.

"Ah. So you noticed his sudden interest in the girl, too?"

Sterling cleared his throat. "I'm sure it's nothing. Q is a big flirt."

"That's one way of putting it," Roger said. "*I* would say that he has a hard time keeping his dick inside his pants."

Okay. This wasn't going to be a friendly conversation.

"The deal was that if he wanted back into the will then he was to agree to marrying Elizabeth Wilde."

"Then perhaps you should remind him," Sterling said.

"That's why I came to you."

Another groan rumbled from Sterling's chest, and he quickly made himself another drink. Why did it always fall on him to get Quentin to toe the line?

"I have a major deal riding on this," his father said. "I need this merger to go through if my company is going to survive this new economy we find ourselves in. Unfortunately, Gregory Wilde, billionaire extraordinaire, wants his daughter to be happy. It's not my fault the disillusioned girl has set her sights on dragging your brother down the aisle, but I *do* plan on delivering him. Lord knows it's not like he's doing anything useful with his life."

Sterling nodded along, even though he didn't completely agree with his father's take on this whole thing. But if Quentin had agreed, then it was up to him to hold up his end of the bargain. "Getting Q to the altar is one thing, his being faithful is another animal completely."

"I'll deal with one crisis at a time." Roger set down his glass and seared him with a leveled gaze. "Talk to him. He won't like it if I have to do it."

Sterling grumbled his understanding.

"Good. I knew that I could count on you." He slapped Sterling on the back and then strolled off to greet his mother and Billy Dee Williams, who rested in the crook of her arm.

Sterling shook his head and then swept his gaze across the growing crowd. He zeroed in on Toni, who was holding Denzel's hand and encouraging him to take a few wobbly steps on his own. His nephew giggled while he discovered the joys of walking.

Jonas and Kerry applauded like a two-member cheerleading squad.

Sterling's heart melted at the sight of them. It would be nice to settle down one day.

"You know that could be you one day," his mother whispered as if she'd plucked the thought out of his head.

Sterling laughed at the sound of his mother's voice breezing across his ear. "Yeah. One day."

"I'm serious," she insisted.

"That's what I'm afraid of."

She frowned and Billy Dee Williams barked as if sensing her displeasure. "Why won't you find yourself a nice girl and settle down? You're just throwing your life away burying your nose in business like you do. Your father and Jonas are both successful and they still manage to raise a family. It just makes me so sad to see you like this."

Billy Dee Williams barked again.

"See. Even Billy agrees with me."

Sterling struggled to keep a cap on his amusement. "You know I have plenty of girlfriends that—"

"No, Mom," Sterling said. "I'm not going to let you and Dad wrangle me into an arranged marriage. It's bad enough that you're doing it to Quentin."

"Oh *that's* different," she huffed. "Quentin is like a ship without a rudder. He just goes in whatever direction the tide takes him."

"It still isn't right."

"Well—" she sighed, not wanting to give an inch "—take it up with your father. He knows better about these things. It's *you* I worry about," she said returning to her original subject.

"Don't worry about me, momma. When the time is right, it'll happen."

She sighed dramatically. "If you say so, dear." She glanced up at him. "But I'll keep my eye out anyway. A woman could never have too many grandbabies."

Sterling's gaze cut back to find Jonas and Toni, but they were gone. Instead, he caught a glimpse of Alyssa in a stunning green gown that made her look like a forest nymph. He marveled at just how beautiful she had turned out to be. He could almost understand Quentin being lured by temptation.

But Alyssa was like a member of the family.

Wasn't she?

"Now there goes trouble," his mother mumbled at his side.

Sterling frowned. "What do you mean?"

"Don't play stupid, son," she said, patting him on the arm. "It doesn't become you."

Alyssa felt nervous as a bride, herself, as she fluttered around the estate, making sure everything was coming along on schedule. She was sure that at any moment the wedding planner was going to evict her. But alas, the guests were seated and the processional music started.

When it was her turn to walk down the aisle, she had the pleasure of linking arms with Roger Hinton, who'd accepted the honor of being her father's best man.

"You look absolutely beautiful," he whispered as they strolled down the aisle.

"Thank you."

Before the preacher, her father smiled down at her with so much love and affection that it nearly overwhelmed her. From the front row on the groom's side, Alyssa felt the heavy weight of Quentin's stare.

Images of them at the pool last night flooded her head. It had been so romantic and so breathtaking that even now she wanted someone to pinch her to make sure that it hadn't all been just a dream. How she had the willpower to stop at just kissing was beyond her. One thing was for sure: it sure as hell hadn't been easy. In fact, when she'd raced back to her room, she felt more like an escaped convict than a woman who had been thoroughly kissed and nearly seduced.

It was the right thing to do, but regret tugged at her.

Alyssa took her place just as the wedding march began.

Estelle made her appearance and everyone climbed to their feet.

Love radiated from her father's eyes, and Alyssa could feel herself growing weepy. By the time the couple linked their arms together and faced the preacher, there wasn't a dry eye in the place. Twenty minutes later, the preacher introduced everyone for the first time to Mr. and Mrs. Alfred Jansen.

"Oh, everything was so beautiful," Tangie cooed as they headed toward the makeshift pavilion. "Do you have a toast prepared?"

"A toast?"

"Yeah. It's customary for the best man and maid of honor to give a toast at the reception."

Alyssa tried not to panic. "I—I guess I'm going to have to wing it," she said. But when she stood to make the toast the words flowed effortlessly. "I've heard that when two people get married, their nuptials have a positive effect on everyone around them. Like someone dropping a pebble into still water, your love sends out ripples of happiness. It brings joy to those who have already said, 'I do,' as they fondly remember their wedding day." She glanced over at Jonas and Toni, and then to her best friend, she added, "It also brings hope to those who are still looking for that special someone.

"Two people brought together by the bonds of love and united in marriage are a powerful force. You bring happiness to those who are here to bear witness and those who couldn't attend, but carry you in their hearts. May your love remain strong to sustain you during times of struggle and enrich the good times you will share together. May it continue to send those ripples of happiness to all of us. Congratulations!"

"Hear, hear!" Everyone raised their glasses.

Next, Mr. Hinton stood and addressed the crowd like a man born on a stage. He recounted the many years her father had worked for him and expressed his unshakable belief that Alfred's next career move would make him the star chef he deserved to be. As always, Roger had a way of talking too much. But it was the end of Roger's speech that finally reeled her back in.

"I hope that everyone will come back here in a couple of months when we'll have another wedding to celebrate," he said.

She glanced up. Who was getting married?

"My son *Quentin* has recently gotten engaged, and his mother and I couldn't be more thrilled."

Alyssa's wineglass slipped from her hand and crashed against the table. All eyes shifted to her.

"Excuse me." She stood and then raced out of the pavilion.

Chapter 10

Quentin cursed under his breath as he cradled his head against the palm of his hand. It took everything he had not to race after Alyssa. Mainly because to do so would definitely get the gossip tongues wagging. His gaze cut back over to his father, who was still standing and holding court. He didn't doubt for a moment that his father made that little announcement specifically for Alyssa's benefit.

For now, all Quentin could do was sit there and stew. When the toast was *finally* over and the music began to play again, an avalanche of congratulations rained down on him. Heavy hands whacked him on the back, while women sent calculating glances his way as if wondering whether he was truly off the market, which in his mind, he wasn't.

As far as he was concerned, this marriage was nothing more than a way for him to ensure his inheritance, since his father had held firm and kept him financially cut off. The question now was how was he going to explain this situation to Alyssa? And he definitely wanted to explain.

After having the taste of her lips more than once, his body now craved more. After seeing the astonished and hurt look on her face, Quentin gave himself a mental kick. Soon the hired waiters came and delivered everyone's meal. Quentin thought this was the perfect time to excuse himself from his table.

Sterling clamped a hand down on his shoulders and stated bluntly. "Let her go. I think you've done enough."

"I have to talk to her."

Sterling shook his head. "And tell her what?"

"You know, you have this annoying habit of putting your nose where it doesn't belong."

Sterling leaned in close. "And you have a habit of thinking with the wrong head."

There were only a few times in Quentin's life when he wanted to punch his brother in the face, mainly because Sterling was much stronger than he was and could kick his butt, but now was one of those times.

"It's none of your business what I do," Quentin hissed. "It's bad enough that I gave my future away so that our old man can get his much-wanted merger.

But I never promised that I would be faithful or a good husband."

"So life goes on as usual. You're going to do whatever the hell you want to do no matter who gets hurt, right? Tell me. What has little Alyssa done for you to think so little of her in all of this?"

"Trust me. I'm thinking about her feelings and everything else if you want me to be honest."

Sterling's jawline hardened. "Careful. If you think for one second that I won't break that glass jaw of yours, you have another thing coming. I won't let you hurt her. She doesn't deserve that kind of treatment from you."

An unmistakable hostility wrapped around the two brothers. No doubt to onlookers it looked as if they were just seconds from throwing the first punch.

"So how is it going over here?" Jonas asked, slapping his hands on each brother's shoulder. "Looks like you two may need a referee."

Sterling and Quentin settled back into their chairs, their gazes still combative.

"We're cool," Q lied, chiseling on a smile. "I was just about to excuse myself."

"Then maybe I should come with you," Sterling said, pushing back his chair.

"Whoa. Whoa," Jonas said, smiling and glancing around to gauge how much attention they were drawing. He leaned closer and hissed. "I don't know what in the hell has gotten into you two, but I suggest that you squash it."

Sterling and Quentin tried to chime in. "But—"

"But nothing," Jonas snapped. "Sit here, smile and act as if you're having a good time."

They both eased back into their chairs.

Just then Alyssa returned to the pavilion. She'd changed her clothes and was now wearing a simple blue dress that made her skin look like rich chocolate.

Quentin's gaze locked on to her while he mentally willed her to look his way.

"Good." Jonas exhaled. "Looks like my work here is done. I expect you two *boys* to behave yourselves." He smiled and then returned to his own table.

Quentin ignored his older brother. All that mattered was him being able to talk with Alyssa— to get her to understand. What he needed was a plan.

A few people at his table tried to engage him in conversation, but he wasn't interested. He could barely do more than nod and shake his head while waiting patiently for Alyssa to spare him a fleeting glance. One look would tell him all he needed to know. Whether he'd lost her before he really had a chance to have her.

It was time for the couple's first dance and Quentin knew his chance was coming. After this, the guests would soon crowd the dance floor and he would be able to get away.

Alyssa watched her father and new stepmother as they glided across the floor to the orchestra's rendition of Nat King Cole's "Unforgettable." Either she was a burgeoning actress or she really didn't give a damn about Quentin anymore.

The thought disheartened him.

The dance came to an end and the crowd applauded. When everyone climbed from their chairs to rush the dance floor, Quentin sprang up, as well. Sterling may have been stronger, but Quentin was quicker.

Threading his way through the crowd tried his patience, but he made it to her table before Antonio could lead her to the dance floor.

"I need to talk to you," he rushed.

"Maybe another time," she said coolly and without looking at him.

"It's important, Alice. I—"

"Stop calling me that," she snapped, her eyes alive with fire. "My name is *not* Alice. It has never been Alice!"

He lurched back in surprise. "I'm sorry. I've upset you."

"I'm not upset," she lied. "Why would I be upset?"

Quentin's gaze shifted to Antonio. "Could you please excuse us for a few minutes?"

Antonio didn't move. Instead, he waited to get the okay from Alyssa.

After a couple of deep, calming breaths, she finally gave him a slow nod.

Antonio marched off, but Quentin clearly saw that his father's driver was none too pleased with him.

"All right. He's gone," she said. "What do you want to talk to me about?"

Quentin looked around and caught his father's gaze. "We should go somewhere so we can talk in private."

"Why? What could you possibly say to me that you can't say right here—or *last night?*"

Quentin cocked his head and tried to bedazzle her with his puppy dog expression. "Please?" He held his breath.

Alyssa stared. Her face washed with doubt, but finally she said, "Two minutes."

"I'll take it."

She stood up from her seat while he came around her table and then looped his arm through hers. When they finally stepped out onto the pavilion, Quentin surprised her by walking her through the evening's cool breeze toward her favorite oak tree. The one she spent most of her childhood climbing. Somewhere on one of the tall branches was both her and Quentin's initials.

"All right, talk," she said, pulling her arm from his and stepping back a bit.

He'd hoped to take her a little farther away, but judging by the look on her face that was out of the question.

"Look, Alice. I know I should have told you about…about…"

"About your engagement?" she filled in for him.

"Yes. About that."

She crossed her arms and tilted her head as though he was now just wasting his time.

"It's not an engagement of love or anything," he started. "It's a little more complicated than that. It's more like an arrangement."

"You're marrying someone you don't love," she asked for clarity.

"Yes."

She waited and then asked. "Why? Is she pregnant or something?"

"No. It's not like that at all. In fact, I hardly know the girl."

Alyssa's delicate brows clashed together. "Come again."

"Well, I've met her once or twice. Like I said it's more like an arrangement."

"What? She's an illegal alien or something?"

"No."

"Will you just spit it out. What kind of arrangement are we talking about?"

Quentin took a deep breath and just went for it. "I'm sure that it's well-known around the grapevine that my father cut me out of his will some time ago and has even cut me off financially. Well, given how much I like to eat and wear clothes, we came up with a little arrangement that would get me back into his good graces."

"You mean this is a *real* arranged marriage…like in the thirteenth century?"

He laughed. "Kind of."

She appeared at a loss for words.

"The last thing I expected was to come back here and find you…to be swept away by you. Trust me when I say this whole thing has taken me by surprise." He moved closer to her and brushed his fingers beneath her chin. "Make no mistake about it…I do *feel* for you…and I want to *be* with you. Will you meet me tonight? Say in about an hour out in the solarium?"

Alyssa stared into Quentin's eyes, feeling every inch of her body melt beneath his intense brown eyes. He wanted her. Tonight she could have him.

"Please," he whispered, pulling her into his embrace. "Please." He lowered his head and once again their lips pressed together and dissolved all doubt in Alyssa's mind. She was floating on that magical cloud again. By the time he drew back, she was breathless and tingly.

"Say you'll meet me in an hour."

Alyssa slowly licked her lips and made her decision. "I'll be there."

Chapter 11

Sterling glided Tangie effortlessly across the dance floor, but his attention wasn't on the beauty in his arms, but on the entrance of the pavilion. *Please, Quentin. Don't do anything stupid.* The words were more than a mantra inside his head, they were a prayer.

True, it had only been a few minutes, but Lord knows it didn't take his brother long to get into trouble. *If he's not back by the end of this song, I'm going out there and dragging him back here.*

As if hearing Sterling's thoughts, Quentin strolled back into the pavilion.

Sterling relaxed.

"What is it?" Tangela asked, stretching her neck around to see what had caught his attention.

"Oh, it's nothing," he lied.

A few seconds later, Alyssa popped back in with her face flushed with new color and her lips swollen as if she'd been thoroughly kissed.

Tension returned to Sterling's shoulders. A renewed anger simmered in his gut. "Ms. Graham, could you excuse me for a moment?" He bowed out of the dance before she had the chance to respond. In just a few smooth strides he made his way across the pavilion and then clamped a hand on Q's arm.

"You're just determined to be hardheaded, aren't you?"

"Me? Hardheaded? Never."

"Don't play games with me."

Ignoring his brother, Quentin casually ordered a drink at the open bar.

"I need to speak with you." Their father suddenly materialized into their small space.

Q rolled his eyes. "I'm sure whatever it is, it can wait. We're at a wedding—or have you two forgotten?" He took his drink from the bartender and started to take a sip when Roger placed his hand over the glass.

"No. It can't wait." Roger's gaze cut to Sterling. "Both of you, in my office—*now.*"

Feeling like an errant child, Sterling marched before his father and led the way back to the main house. By the time he eased into the burgundy chair next to his father's desk, his temper was nearly volcanic.

Quentin, on the other hand, entered the office cool

as a cucumber, his stroll overly confident, his eyes twinkling and his grin too cocky by half.

"If I was you, I wouldn't try me, boy," his father warned. "Sit down."

As if to prove a point, Q remained standing while his father shuffled around his desk and then plopped into his chair.

"Do you really want to try me?" Roger asked in a dangerous *Dirty Harry* voice.

Quentin swallowed hard, but he made his way into the chair.

Roger straightened and kept his hardened stare on his youngest son. "Now, I don't know what kind of game you're playing but when you start messing with my money, you're messing with my emotions— and I will *not* stand for it." He slammed a fist onto his desk. "I need to know right now, do we or do we *not* have a deal regarding your pending nuptials?"

Quentin hesitated, shifted in his chair.

"Before you answer," their father continued, "let me make myself clear. This is the *final* chance I'm giving you. I've given you plenty of chances to get your act together. But all you seem to think is that life is one big party. I sent you to the best schools, gave you cushy positions in my companies. Hell, your brothers have even tried to whip you into shape."

Uncomfortable in witnessing this, Sterling dropped his gaze and braided his hands.

"So, I cut you off. Hoped that would send a clear message that it's time for you to grow up. Be responsible. Why can't you be more like your brothers? They've made a name for themselves—launched successful companies one after another. Instead, you prefer to have women pay your way. Back in my day we had a name for that. And it certainly wasn't anything to be proud of."

Quentin's cocky smile disappeared.

"Then finally, like I knew eventually you would, you came crawling back. And I—" he leaned back in his chair and covered his hands across his chest "—being the good father that I am, gave you one more chance."

"And under one condition," Quentin reminded him.

"*Everything* has conditions." Roger leveled with him. "I would have thought that you would have learned that by now."

For a long while, the office fell as silent as a tomb.

"Now!" Roger sat forward again and steepled his fingers together. "I've laid all my cards on the table. You *know* how much this merger means to my company. These are hard economic times we're living in and I have too much riding on this. But if you back out, I swear by all that is holy that your mother and I will make sure you'll never see one dime from this estate. Do I make myself clear?"

Their gazes warred with each other.

"You think I'm bluffing?" Roger asked.

Both brothers knew that their father *never* bluffed.

Sterling finally looked at his brother again, who seemed to have shrunk in his seat.

"I want an answer," Roger pressed.

At last, Quentin dropped his head and mumbled.

"I can't hear you."

Quentin swallowed his pride and lifted his chin. "I *said* we have a deal."

"Good." Roger smiled. "I knew that you'd come around." He finally glanced over at Sterling. "Your brother here can make your apologies to Alyssa in the solarium. I'm sure she'll understand."

Quentin's eyebrows spiked in surprise. "How did you—?"

"What?" Roger shrugged, standing up. "You think I don't know everything that goes on around here? I have eyes and ears *everywhere*. You're not going. Sterling will handle it."

"Me?"

Roger glanced toward Sterling. "Problem?"

Sterling's irritation mounted. Once again he was being sent to clean up Quentin's mess.

"You—" Roger turned back toward Quentin "—have other things to tend to."

"Like what?"

"Like your fiancée. I called the Wildes and let them know that you were in town. Told them to come over and join the party."

"You invited them to crash a wedding?"

"I'm sure that Alfred and Estelle won't mind."

That shifty move even surprised Sterling.

"Besides, there's no time like the present for you two to get to know each other." He walked around his desk and laid a hand against Q's shoulder. "And what better place to do that than at a wedding? It's even kind of romantic."

Quentin shook his head. "You've gone too far."

"Have I? Or maybe I should let you risk everything so you can chase after a servant's daughter?" The hostility returned to his voice. "That girl has been running around here since she was five or six. Do you have *no* shame?"

For the first time, Quentin colored.

"Sterling," their father barked.

"Yes, sir?"

"Please send Alyssa Quentin's regrets, but at the moment he's indisposed with his fiancée for the rest of the evening."

Dread crawled up Sterling's spine. "Yes, sir." He climbed to his feet and noticed how his brother refused to look at him. He marched out of the office.

As he made his way back outside, he thought how disconcerting it was for his father to still be barking out orders at them. But in this case, he agreed with his father. Quentin was being more than a little careless and predatory toward a woman he knew full well harbored childhood fantasies about him. That kind of behavior was unforgivable.

He only hoped that Alyssa handled the news well.

Exiting the main garden, Sterling was instantly greeted with the haunting tune of "Unforgettable." The beautiful music dusted off some more feelings that he was trying to ignore. There was nothing like a wedding to help Sterling realize how lonely he was. Weddings had a way of making you stop and take stock of your life.

By the time he reached the pavilion, he was humming along with the song. On the dance floor, he saw couples rocking back and forth, smiling. Everyone still seemed to be having a good time. His gaze then skimmed the crowd and he realized that he'd missed Alfred and Estelle's departure for their honeymoon.

He smiled, thinking of Alfred. He truly hoped his friend fulfilled his dreams.

"Unforgettable" ended and the orchestra launched into a string version of Luther Vandross's "Any Love."

Sterling's loneliness returned. "One bottle of champagne and two glasses." He stuffed money into the bartender's tip jar, and then accepted the bottle and glasses. Alcohol always eased bad news, he reasoned.

As he headed toward the solarium, he felt like a dead man walking.

When he finally arrived at what most referred to as his mother's sanctuary, he took a deep breath and entered. The music was clear and a sliver of moonlight cast the flowers and plants in an ethereal romantic glow.

"Quentin?" Alyssa's soft voice drifted from behind a tall plant. When she stepped out into view, it was like a star stepping out into the spotlight.

Sterling sucked in a small gasp. She seemed to grow more beautiful each time he laid eyes on her. How was that possible?

"Oh, Sterling." She smiled awkwardly. "I thought you were someone else."

He smiled. "I kind of gathered that." He stepped forward, hating more than ever that he was the bearer of bad news. "I'm sorry to have disappointed you, but um…"

"He's not coming. Is he?"

Sterling drew in a deep breath and then slowly shook his head. "I'm sorry."

"I see."

After a long silence Sterling felt the need to fill it. "Something's…come up."

She nodded absently, but at the same time, she looked so small. Was she embarrassed?

"He wanted me to send his apologies."

"Did he now? Or did your father send you?"

Sterling didn't know what to say. For a few seconds, the music just drifted between them.

"What do you have there?" She straightened her shoulders.

Sterling had forgotten about the champagne. "I, um, maybe we could share a drink."

Alyssa smiled. "You always were the nice one."

"And nice guys always finish last," he joked.

Her smile broadened with a hint of sympathy. "That's not always true."

They smiled.

"So how about it?" he asked. "Want to share a drink with an old friend?"

"Are we?" Their gazes locked. "Friends?"

"I've always thought so."

"Really?" she asked dubiously. "You don't look at me and see me as just the servant's daughter?"

"No." But he had hesitated.

Her smile melted. "Maybe I *need* that drink." She reached for the bottle, and when her hand brushed his, there was this weird staticlike spark that caused his whole arm to tingle. Out of reflex, he stepped back.

"I'll open it," he said, covering his reaction. He handed her the glasses while he worked the bottle's cork.

Maybe it was the music or even the moonlight, but Sterling was suddenly nervous being alone with his...*friend.*

The cork popped and a small rush of champagne bubbled over the top.

"Whoa." He laughed.

A smiling Alyssa held up their glasses while he filled them. He placed the bottle down on a stone ledge and took his glass.

"So what should we drink to?" Alyssa asked. "My making a fool of myself?"

"Of course not," he admonished. "You're being too hard on yourself. Quentin is very charming."

Silence, and then, "Is he really getting married?"

Sterling stared. Her dark gaze shimmered beneath the moonlight. "Yes."

"Does he love her?"

Sterling started to answer, but she stopped him.

"Don't answer that." She laughed and shook her head. "It really doesn't matter."

"Why don't we toast to you?" he asked, and then lifted his glass. "To your success, your independence. You've come a long way from being that cute little girl climbing everything that stood still."

She laughed and then clinked her glass against his. "Thank you." She sipped her champagne while the orchestra played "Isn't It Romantic?"

"Care to dance?" Sterling asked, holding out his hand.

Alyssa chuckled. "I never thought of you as much of a dancer."

"I'm not." He shrugged. "But I can rock back and forth pretty good."

"All right." She set her glass down and then glided into his open arms.

Sterling led her in a slow two-step while he hummed in tune. His seductive baritone caused Alyssa to close her eyes and drift in the moment.

Sure, she was disappointed that Quentin hadn't come, but there was a strange sort of comfort being there with Sterling. She felt safe and…what? There was something warm and…magical about the evening.

About this moment.

She joined him in his humming and their soft duet actually sounded pretty good. Maybe everything had worked out for the best. In the morning, she'd be gone and she could finally put her childhood fantasy behind her.

The song ended. Alyssa gently stepped out of Sterling's embrace. "Thanks. I appreciate you being a good friend. Like always."

"Anytime."

"Good night." She smiled and then leaned up on her toes and pressed a kiss against his cheek.

"Night." Sterling watched her turn and walk away, his cheek tingling.

Dollhouse Confessions

Chapter 12

Now...

Quentin drew in a deep breath. "I should have gone to her that night," he said with a long sigh of disgust. "All my life I'd never bowed to the whims of my father—but that time I allowed him to jerk my chain."

Xavier poured himself another drink. "Sounds like she really got under your skin."

"She did."

"What makes you think that things would have worked out any different with her than any other woman you've dated over the years? Maybe it was just your pride that was at stake."

Quentin pressed a hand against his bruised face. "I think I'm losing feeling on this side."

Xavier laughed. "You're avoiding the question."

Quentin lowered his hand and tried his best to smile. "You know me too well."

His cousin shrugged and leaned back in his chair, but he still waited for his answer.

"Maybe it was my pride," Quentin confessed. "At least at first. I mean she's beautiful and is literally splashed over every major magazine."

"So she was a conquest?"

"Yes—no." Quentin thought it over. "I'm not sure. I just know that I can't get her out my head."

Xavier sipped his drink. "So what did you do?"

"I didn't *do* anything. I just went on about my life. Did what my daddy told me. I married Elizabeth. Not Lizzy or Liz or even Beth." He smirked at his cousin. "She hated nicknames."

Xavier laughed heartily. "I remember the marriage. I was invited to the wedding. Remember? Course, I was surprised it lasted as long as it did. Six months is nothing to sneeze at."

"I thought so."

"It was pretty funny…at least on my end. My brother thought you wouldn't last past the honeymoon."

Quentin chuckled. "I almost didn't."

"You're kidding."

"Well, at the hotel, there was this one chick—"

"You know what? I don't even want to know."

Xavier laughed, tossing up his hands. "You might want to look into therapy."

"All right. I admit it. It's not easy for me to be faithful to *one* woman."

"Then why stress over this Alyssa. By all accounts, it would have ended the same way as all the others."

Quentin fell silent. He brooded.

"Okay," Xavier said, seeing that angle wasn't getting him anywhere. "Your divorce was years ago. Why didn't you just look Alyssa up?"

"I did…eventually. But by that time, someone had beaten me to the punch—my overprotective brother, Sterling."

Chapter 13

Three years ago...

Sterling couldn't remember the last time he was sick. It might have been as far back as elementary school. That wasn't the case today. Today he felt like he'd been run over by a Mack truck. His head ached, his eyes watered, his throat felt scratchy, and he coughed so much he was sure everything would be all right once he finally coughed up his pesky lungs.

More importantly, he just wished that someone would take him out of his misery. Buried beneath a mountain of blankets, while a humidifier filled the room with Vicks VapoRub, Sterling thought that he had finally found the perfect spot in the king-size bed where he could drift off into a nice NyQuil coma when his phone rang.

Groaning in agony, Sterling tossed a pillow over his head and tried to block out the world. "Leeeave meee aalooone," he whined.

Whoever it was wouldn't leave him alone. They would just hang up and call back instead of leaving a message on the answer machine. Finally to prevent himself from going insane, he shot out an arm and snatched up the phone.

"Whaaat?"

"Sterling?" Toni questioned. "My God you sound awful."

"Thank you," he said. "What do you want?" He wasn't interested in being cordial and at this moment, he just wanted to hurry and get off the phone and return to his deep sleep.

"I forgot the code to the gate."

He frowned. "You're here?"

"Yes. It's me and the kids, we brought you some soup."

The kids. They were the ones who'd gotten him sick in the first place. He was on the verge of telling her to go away when the idea of soup caused his stomach to rumble. But wouldn't that mean he would have to get out of bed? Frankly, he'd rather starve than move. "I don't know, Toni. I really am feeling kind of beat."

"Which is why you need someone to take care of you."

He didn't answer.

"C'mon, Sterling. It's freezing out here. Buzz us in."

"All right. All right," he said after another series of groans. He punched in the code for the gate and then tried to hang up the phone, but after several failed attempts, he just dropped the handset and let it dangle by the cord attached to the phone on the nightstand. He told himself to get up, but damned if he could manage it. His limbs had to weigh at least a thousand pounds.

He started drifting back off to sleep when he heard the sounds of children bursting into the house.

"Uncle Sterling! Uncle Sterling!" Kerry's voice screeched down the hallway.

"Where are you? Uncle Sterling?" Denzel called. The sound of his little feet racing against the hard-wood floor did elicit a weak smile.

In the next second his bedroom door burst open and Kerry announced, "He's in here!"

Sterling pried open his eyes just as Toni entered the room and flipped on the light switch. It was like a million daggers stabbing the back of his eyes. He squeezed them shut again and moaned, "Cut it off. Please. Cut it off." He grabbed a pillow and pulled it over his head.

Kerry launched up on the four-poster bed. Her bony knees stabbed him in his sides.

"Oof."

"Uncle Sterling, what's wrong?" she asked, prying the pillow away and slapping her hand against his forehead. "Momma, he's hot."

"I want up," Denzel complained.

"Here. I got you," Kerry said, grabbing his arm and tugging him onto the bed.

Now it was his nephew's turn to start crawling all over him like he was a human jungle gym.

"Oh, Lord. You guys are killing me," Sterling mumbled. But the kids paid no heed to his protest.

Denzel reached up and lifted his uncle's right eyelid with his finger. "Are you trying to sleep, Uncle Sterling?"

"I was."

"Kids, please leave your uncle alone. He doesn't feel well," Toni said.

The delicious scent of chicken noodle soup wafted through the bedroom and Sterling's stomach growled.

Kerry and Denzel erupted into giggles.

"How did you do that?" Denzel asked, dropping his ear against Sterling's belly, and waited for a second growl.

"Goodness. How long have you been in here like this? That Vicks stuff is singeing my nose," she complained. She also pressed her hand against his forehead. "You *are* burning up."

"Just go away and leave me here to die in peace."

She laughed. "Talk about being a big baby. You and Jonas have that in common when you're sick."

"Where's my pillow?"

"Kids, climb down. Kerry, go in the kitchen and see if there's some orange juice in the refrigerator and pour your uncle a glass."

"Yes, ma'am," she said, jumping off the bed, and racing out of the room.

"Why don't you feel good, Uncle Sterling?" Denzel inquired. "Here. Take Mr. Wiggles. He'll make you feel better." He shoved his tattered teddy bear under Sterling's arm. "He always makes me feel better, doesn't he, momma?"

"That's right, baby." Toni kissed her son's cheek. "C'mon, Sterling. Sit up. I want you eat some of this soup." She shut off the humidifier and then glanced around. "Where do you keep your serving trays?"

He huffed and tried to think. "In the kitchen."

"Denzel, go tell your sister to bring me a serving tray."

"Yes, momma."

Toni helped him down from the bed and then watched him race out of the room.

"Kerry!"

"Denzel! No yelling," Toni shouted after him.

Sterling's head exploded. Were they there to help him or kill him?

"Do you have a thermometer?" she asked, busying herself around the room.

"Bathroom, medicine cabinet."

She headed to the bathroom, tsking under her breath. "Why didn't you call and tell me that you were sick?"

"Really. It's nothing I can't handle," he said, trying to pull himself up. "It's just a cold."

"Humph!" She walked back into the room. "You look like death warmed over."

"You know you shouldn't try so hard to make me feel better."

"It's the least I can do." She smiled. "Now open your mouth."

He complied and she shoved the thermometer under his tongue.

"Now, see. This is why you need a woman around. You need someone to take care of you when your Superman suit is in the cleaners. It's okay to admit you need someone. Trust me. I had to learn the hard way."

"We're not back on that are we?"

"Of course we are. It's waaay past time for you to settle down."

He shook his head. "I swear you are sounding more and more like my mother."

"Well, have you thought that *maybe* your mother is right?"

Sterling rolled his eyes.

"I mean I don't understand why you're still single. You're handsome, rich, kind. Women should be throwing themselves at you." She cocked her head. "Maybe they are and you're just not noticing them?"

"Relationships are complicated," he said.

"But rewarding," she countered. "Trust me. I used to put up a lot of roadblocks myself back in the day." As if suddenly remembering their brief relationship, she felt her gaze jump up to his, and the room filled with an awkward tension.

They were saved by the beeping thermometer.

"My gosh. You're really burning up."

"I wanna carry it," Denzel whined out in the hallway.

"Here," Kerry said. "But don't spill it."

"I won't." And then a second later. "Ooops."

Toni rolled her eyes. "Sounds like I have another mess to clean up."

A few minutes later, Toni had Sterling propped up in bed with his breakfast tray and a hot steaming bowl of soup and half a glass of orange juice. At his side, his niece and nephew argued over the TV remote while Toni scampered around picking up.

"I wanna have it."

"No."

"Uncle Sterliiinng…"

"It's okay, Kerry. Let him have it."

None too happy, she let her brother take the remote and switch the channel from her much-beloved Disney Channel. Now they had to endure Denzel going from one channel to another at warp speed.

Sterling really didn't care. The soup was hitting the right spot as far as he was concerned and he couldn't stop from moaning with every spoonful. Absently, he glanced up at the TV and caught sight of a familiar face.

"Whoa. Whoa. Go back. Go back."

Denzel looked confused with the order.

Sterling reached over and gently claimed the remote and flipped back a couple of channels. He landed on a talk show and a smile spread across his face. "Well, I'll be."

Alyssa Jansen smiled broadly back at him through the television screen.

"Ooh. She's pretty," Kerry said, plopping on her belly and cradling her head with her hands. "I like her hair."

"So," the television hostess asked, "do you have any advice to the young women out there that might want to get into the modeling business?"

Alyssa's luminous smile sparkled. "Well, first I would suggest the young ladies think really long and hard about it. It's harder than it looks. Then if it's something that you really want to do then the name of the game is to get with a good reputable modeling agency."

"I have a juicy question I'd like to ask," the pert hostess said.

Alyssa shifted in her chair, but her smile remained.

"With being one of the most sought-after models in the industry right now, do you have anyone special in your life?"

An adorable blush crept into Alyssa's face and Sterling found himself smiling at the television screen.

"C'mon, girl. You can tell us," the hostess coerced in her best sister-girl persona. "We won't tell nobody, right?"

Everyone in the audience cheered.

The camera cut back to Alyssa whose embarrassment grew by leaps and bounds. "There's… someone," she admitted.

"Oooh," the audience chimed in unison and then broke out into a round of applause.

"Can I watch Disney now?" Kerry asked.

"Sure." Sterling handed her the remote, but his mind remained on Alyssa. Whoever she was seeing, he was one lucky son of a bitch.

Chapter 14

"I can't believe you lied on national TV," Tangie laughed, following Alyssa through the door of her swanky Malibu home. In the past few years, the dynamics of the best friend's relationship had changed. Tangie had gone from being her assistant to being her agent.

"What—you thought I was going to tell the whole world that I haven't so much as been on a date in ten months?" Alyssa laughed. "Thanks, but no thanks."

"Well whose fault is that?" Tangie harped. "I've been telling you not to take *every* job offered for a while now."

"That's because you don't see the big picture," she said. "These jobs are what's going to help launch my new clothing line next year. The more money I put into it and not the investors, the more control I have."

"And when will you have time to promote the perfume line?"

"Don't worry, boss. I have it all under control," she said, heading into the kitchen. "Just call me Superwoman."

Tangie settled a hand against her waist. "All right, *Superwoman,* where's your man at?"

"Fine. You made your point." Alyssa pulled open the refrigerator and removed a prepared meal left by her nutritionist that would undoubtedly have about the same amount of flavor as it had calories. "So what do you suggest I do, Dr. Love? You're the one with the ring on her finger. How do I go about finding Mr. Right?"

"Well, he certainly isn't going to just pop up and ring your doorbell," she chastised.

The doorbell rang.

The women glanced at each other with a "who's that?" look.

It turned out to be the UPS man. While Alyssa signed for her delivery, she and Tangie exchanged bemused looks.

"So," Tangie said, crossing her arms, "how long have you been a deliveryman?"

The driver, who couldn't take his eyes off Alyssa, puffed out his chest. "Four years."

"Thank you," Alyssa said, handing back his electronic pad and then gently closing the door in his face.

"See? *That's* why you can't get a man."

"He had a wedding band on."

"But is he happy?"

Alyssa's head rocked back with laughter. "Girl, you ain't right." She marched back to the kitchen.

"Don't underestimate married men. They're the only ones up in the club acting like everything is everything."

"What is your married butt doing up in the club?"

"See what I mean?"

"If that's what you and Craig call a marriage, then no thank you."

"I give up," Tangie said, tossing up her hands and then retrieving a bottle of wine. "Want some?"

"Sure. Why not?" She picked through her cold bean and alfalfa concoction. She sat quiet for a moment. Except when Tangie came over, her house was always quiet. In her head she remembered the time when she seriously considered going after Quentin when she *knew* that he was heading toward the altar. It had been a moment of weakness. After all, Quentin had been a childhood fantasy and it was like dangling a carrot before a starving rabbit. "Maybe I should get a dog or something?"

"A dog is nice." Tangela poured their wine. "But it's not a man."

"Dog, man. Man, dog." Alyssa shrugged, smiling. "What's the difference?"

"If you don't know, then you're worse off than I thought."

Alyssa just smiled sheepishly.

"The problem is that you're too picky. This one is too tall. That one is too short. This guy lives with his mother and that guy looks in the mirror too much."

"A woman should never compete with a man hogging a mirror."

"Have you forgotten where you live? Ninety percent of the men are either models or actors or want to be both."

"And I don't want to have anything to do with any of them." She frowned and took a bite of her food. "I want a regular Joe. I don't think I could ever be with someone in this business. I can see myself with a regular pencil pusher."

"Numbers and spreadsheets, huh?"

"Maybe a lawyer."

"There're lawyers here."

"There're slimeballs here," Alyssa corrected.

"That's what I said."

Alyssa shoved more alfalfa sprouts into her mouth. "I know one thing. Once I make the transition from supermodel to businesswoman, I'm going to start eating real food. People are going to do those 'Where are they now' searches and see me looking as big as a house."

Tangie laughed.

"I'm serious. Do you know how long it's been since I had fried chicken, macaroni and cheese—hell, peach cobbler." She groaned and collapsed against the counter; her eyes rolled back.

"You *could* cheat every once in a while."

Alyssa sat up. "Can't. One slip and I'm afraid I'm a goner. And visiting my dad is just like slow torture. He always cooks enough food to feed the entire state of Georgia. And then I'm standing there like an idiot chomping on carrots or celery while everything smells wonderful. Once, I did *sneak* a butter roll and I swear I had an orgasm."

"That is so sad. And I'm going to put that in my TMI file, if you don't mind."

"The bottom line is there's something to retiring on top in this industry. Cindy Crawford did it, Iman, Tyra Banks."

"Whatever, girl. I guess that means that I better pump up my list if I'm going to be losing my top client."

"Yep. I'm going to be a regular businesswoman and soccer mom."

"You keep skipping steps. You have to be a wife before becoming a soccer mom."

"We keep coming back to that, huh?"

"Afraid so."

She sighed. "Dating would be a lot easier if men weren't allowed to talk."

"Amen." Tangie lifted her glass for an impromptu toast.

Sterling was out like a light.

And in his dreams, he kept seeing images of Alyssa's smiling face on the television screen. *"Do you have anyone special in your life?"* the hostess asked again.

"Yes, I'm seeing this really great guy that I've known most of my life—Sterling Hinton." Alyssa answered. She kissed her fingers and then blew a kiss to the camera. I love you, baby."

Sterling smiled and shuffled under the blanket. There was something ringing somewhere and he grew irritated that the television hostess wouldn't stop to answer it.

The ringing grew louder and louder. Finally it sank into his head that the ringing wasn't a part of the dream. It was the phone.

Groaning and wrestling his way out from his warm cocoon, he wrenched the phone off the hook. "What?"

"Bro," Quentin shouted. "What the hell's wrong with you? You sound awful."

"I'm sick."

"Still?"

"Go away and call me later," he ordered grumpily.

"I can't. I'm at the gate. Did you change the code or something?"

"Yeah," he lied. Quentin rarely committed anything to memory. "I'm trying to keep freeloaders out."

"You're a regular Chris Rock. Now buzz me in. It's cold out here."

Why couldn't everybody just leave him alone?

"Hello? You still there?" Quentin asked.

"All right. All right." Sterling punched in the code and then slammed the phone down. Lord, save him from concerned family members. In a snap, he was asleep again. But five minutes later, his brother was standing over him and pushing up his eyelid.

"Yo, man. Wake up."

Sterling slapped his hand away. "Money's in wallet. Go away."

"I didn't come to hit you up…but if you're offering."

Sterling groaned.

"Man, what's that burning my nose hairs?" He picked up a jar. "Vicks? What are you, twelve?"

"Did you miss the part when I said I was sick?"

Quentin plopped down on the bed, narrowly missing Sterling's legs. "That's just it. I can't remember you ever being sick." He slapped a hand across Sterling's forehead. "You feel all right to me."

"Is there something you want?" Sterling shoved his hand away. "I'd like to go back to dying here in peace, if you don't mind." He started coughing and the next thing he knew, he was hacking and his entire chest started hurting.

"Easy there. Easy. Don't die on me."

"What do you want?"

"I wanted to talk to you." Quentin responded in an upbeat voice. "You'll never guess who I saw on television today."

Sterling didn't know nor did he care.

"C'mon, guess."

"I don't know, Q. Goooo away."

Quentin bounced on the bed. "Guess."

Clearly he wasn't going to get any rest until he played this game. "All right. Dad was on TV."

"Would I be excited about seeing Dad? You know he hasn't spoken to me since the divorce."

"Mom," Sterling tried again.

"Nope."

"I give up."

"Think of a beautiful enchantress that's splashed over every magazine cover."

Sterling's eyes opened. He knew, but didn't answer.

"Alice Jansen," Quentin proudly announced.

"Her name is Alyssa."

"She may be Alyssa to you, but she'll always be *my* Alice."

Sterling rolled his eyes and then grabbed a pillow and plopped it over his head. The last thing he wanted to hear was Q pining about what could have been with Alyssa.

"Alice was on this talk show earlier," Q continued, snatching the pillow from his brother's head. "My God, bro. You should have seen her. I swear she gets more beautiful every time I see her. I should've pursued her when I had a chance. Instead I let you and Dad bully me into marrying Lizzie."

"Elizabeth."

"Whatever."

"And I didn't bully you into marrying Elizabeth. You agreed to that all on your own."

"That's not how I remember it."

"Why am I not surprised?"

"Alice was the one I should have married. I just can't get her out of my mind."

Sterling finally pushed himself up. "I don't believe I'm hearing this."

"It's true and you know it's true. She's the one."

"And she makes enough money to support both of you."

Quentin's shoulders deflated. "You cut me deep, bro. You cut me deep."

"I'm going back to sleep." He dived back under the covers and hoped his brother would pick up the hint.

He didn't. Q snatched back the covers. "I was hoping that you could help me."

Sterling groaned.

"I know you've kept up with Alfred since he left Dad's employ—maybe even Alice."

"No."

"Now you're just being mean."

"Fine. I'm being mean. Now go away."

"Sterling."

Sterling sat up. "Do you think I'm actually going to feed Alfred's daughter to you? The longest relationship you have ever had was your six-month marriage. The answer is not just no, but oh-hell-no!"

"Sterling—"

"I'm sick, but I'm not crazy."

Quentin looked genuinely hurt. "Whatever happened to blood being thicker than water?"

"Q, forget about Alyssa Jansen. You're not programmed for monogamy. Besides, she said that she's seeing someone."

"How did you—did you see the show?"

Sterling sighed. He'd said too much.

Quentin's eyes narrowed. "You know, I've always been suspicious of what happened that night between you two in the solarium."

Sterling blinked. "Are you for real?"

Q crossed his arms.

"Okay, now I know that you're crazy, though all evidence pointing to that conclusion occurred some time ago. Alyssa is like...an adopted sister or a cousin. She grew up around us."

"All right. Fine. I'll find her without your help." He stood up and reached for his brother's wallet on the nightstand. "And since you offered..."

Sterling shook his head.

"Xavier and I are going skiing this weekend. As soon as I get back, I'm hot on Alice's trail. Trust me, I'm going to find her, and when I do, I'm making her the next Mrs. Hinton."

Chapter 15

This Christmas Alfred was determined to win the Christmas nativity and decorations competition in his subdivision. He'd already invested a fortune in Christmas lights. This past fall, he made mountains of sketches of exactly what he wanted to pull off. This year his baby, Jessica, was finally old enough to appreciate the wonders of Santa Claus and Christmas presents and glowing lights.

Alyssa used to love the holidays, too. He was glad that his older daughter still made time in her busy schedule to fly to Atlanta so that they could all be one big, happy family. He'd been married a few years now and the whole family life suited him well again.

"Now you be careful up there," Estelle warned, watching him crawl across the roof.

"I'm always careful, dear," he said, smiling. Alfred had to admit that it felt good to have someone worry about him like this, just as it felt good to be able to love and cherish again. *Forgive me, Melissa.*

Most days, Alfred had to pinch himself. His cooking show was a great success. He was in syndication in twenty-five major cities. His third cookbook was steadily climbing up the best seller's list on the *NY Times* and he now was in talks about developing his own cookware. Everything was going great, though Estelle often complained that he worked too much.

Maybe he did. But he had so much he wanted to do and accomplish. It wasn't because he regretted all those years working at the Hinton estate, because he didn't. But now was his time. And the one person that truly inspired him was his own daughter Alyssa.

"Well I'm going inside to make you some hot cider," Estelle said. "You're going to be freezing when you get finished."

"All right, dear."

"Don't stay out here too long. It's supposed to freeze tonight."

"Yes, dear." Alfred smiled and continued on with his sketches and staple gun.

A strong gust of wind blew from the east, numbing Alfred's fingers and nose. Suddenly a strange tingling shot up his arm, and then the tingling began to hurt. He dropped the staple gun.

"Oh God." Pain exploded in his chest and Alfred lost his footing. He fell and then rolled off the roof.

Alyssa hopped the first flight out of LAX to Atlanta. The entire time, her stomach was tied into a tight knot.

She felt weak.

She felt hot.

She felt panicked.

A heart attack, her stepmother had said. How could such a thing be possible? Her father had to be one of the strongest people she knew. She couldn't imagine such a thing befalling him. It just couldn't be, she kept saying to herself, but it wasn't working.

Alyssa's heart sank like a stone.

"It's going to be all right," Tangie whispered, grabbing her hand and squeezing it tight. "You'll see. He'll come through this."

Alyssa tried to smile, but she couldn't.

A few people swiveled in their chairs to stare at her. There was a celebrity in their midst.

She reached into her purse and retrieved her large sunglasses, hoping to hide from the onlookers. Even that wasn't working.

C'mon. C'mon, she mentally urged the plane to hurry. She had to get to her father. Surely once she reached his side everything would be all right.

Just hang in there, Daddy.

The five-hour flight seemed more like twenty. She felt like weeping when the plane's wheels finally touched down. Alyssa and Tangela rushed through the terminals and hopped on the concourse to the rental car line. The aggravating part was when they had finally reached Grady Hospital and the nurses couldn't find what room her father was in. For the first time in her life, Alyssa threw a major temper tantrum, and Estelle appeared and rescued the poor medical staff.

"It's okay. She's with me." Estelle took her by the hand and led her to her father's room.

Despite what she thought, Alyssa was totally unprepared to see a shell of her father nestled in a bed of white sheets. In fact, it took a few heartbeats before she even recognized him. There were tubes in his mouth and arms. There were bruises on his face and his dark coloring looked more gray than black.

And he looked so incredibly weak.

"Oh, Daddy." Alyssa rushed to the bed, but was careful not to disturb the butterfly needle in his hand. "My God. What happened to you?"

A monitor beeped steadily nearby. She glanced at it and tried to make sense of the lines and numbers.

Tangie pulled a chair up to the bed for her.

"I came as fast as I could, Dad. Now you start trying to get better."

Estelle sobbed in the corner, but Alyssa couldn't spare her a glance.

Alyssa gently laced her fingers in between her father's and tried to mentally will him to open his eyes. However, the only sound in the room was the steady beep of the heart monitor and the soft whirl of the air conditioner.

It was sad.

It was pathetic.

But right now—it was enough for her. Now that she was here, she was certain her father would pull through. He just had to. She lifted his hand and placed it against her cheek. It was cold and almost lifeless. Tears streamed steadily down her face while her emotions continued to clog her throat.

The long hours turned into troubling days. The numbers and constant news from the doctors became more grave.

On the third day, Alfred's heartbeat flatlined.

Sterling was shocked when he got the news. And he wasn't the only one. Roger Hinton was more than a little choked up when he delivered the news. Alfred Jansen had been more than a great employee to the Hintons. He was a great man...and friend. After his father relayed the time and date for the funeral, Sterling promised that he would be there despite his lingering cold.

When Sterling ended the call, his thoughts instantly traveled to Alyssa. How was she handling the news? Something told him not too well. His heart went out to her.

Two days later, Sterling sat in a crowded pew of the Atlanta Baptist Church. Despite the singing and the moving sermon from the reverend, the mood remained somber. One by one, people stood and shared stories of a man as big as a lion but with the heart of a kitten.

In the front, Alyssa, dressed in black, listened to the stories with a soft smile but with tears sliding down her face. Even then she was a remarkable beauty that drew everyone's eye.

Estelle, however, was a wreck.

When the reverend asked if anyone else wanted to speak, Sterling stood and walked solemnly down the aisle. At the podium, he looked out among the large crowd and felt his throat tighten with emotion. Luckily, he'd written down everything he'd wanted to say because at that moment his mind was a blank.

Standing there with an escalating fever, Sterling struggled to keep his voice level. He recalled how he knew Alfred and shared a few personal stories. Many were humorous and some downright touching. "Alfred was a great man," he proclaimed and then looked at Alyssa, "and a great friend. I will miss him dearly."

He stepped down from the podium and headed back to his seat. As he started past Alyssa's pew, she reached out for his hand and stopped him.

"Thank you," she whispered.

Sterling met her watery gaze and his heart tugged again. He gave her a slight nod and then returned to his seat in time to hear his father.

An hour later, everyone had gathered at the fresh grave site to say their goodbyes. Light snow flurries whipped around the crowd, while the blustering wind turned arctic. The mourners huddled together and watched as the black casket descended into the earth.

Estelle slumped against Alyssa, who looked no better prepared for the added weight than a pile of toothpicks.

Sterling walked over to them and took Estelle by the hand. She looked up at him and then transferred her weight to his strong shoulders.

Alyssa's grateful gaze landed on him. "Thank you," she mouthed.

Again, he just nodded and continued listening to the burial rites.

As the family walked to the waiting limos, Sterling continued offering Estelle his shoulder while Alyssa carried her younger sister on her hip.

"Thank you again," Alyssa said, once her small family settled into their seat. She stood outside by her open door, looking as frail as she had that night in the solarium.

"Anytime," he said. "How are *you* holding up?"

"I'm not sure. I'm still hoping my alarm clock is going to go off, and all of this is just some horrible dream."

His shoulders deflated. "I'm sorry." He opened his arms and without hesitating, she slid into them. As he folded his arms around her, he swore there was something like a click inside his head and the world suddenly faded away. He kissed the top of her head. "Is there anything I can do?"

She shook her head and then slowly eased out of his arms. "No. I think I'll be all right."

Sterling reached into his breast pocket and pulled out a card. "If you change your mind, give me a call. Anytime."

"Thanks. I just might take you up on that."

Chapter 16

For the next two days, Alyssa and Estelle did their best to console each other. But after going through a record number of Kleenex boxes, they began to question whether they were comforting each other or prolonging their grief. They moved like ghosts around each other with long faces and puffy red eyes.

The hardest part for both of them was to listen to little Jessica constantly ask when her daddy was going to be finished with his nap. There was a sad irony that didn't escape Alyssa. She'd lost her mother when she was only four and here Jessica had lost her father at almost the same age.

Life could be cruel.

It broke her heart to know that there was the possibility that Jessica would only remember her father through pictures and stories from her older sister. More tears welled in Alyssa's eyes as she reached for another tissue.

The box was empty.

"Would you like for me to fix you something else to eat?" Estelle asked, leaning against the living room archway. "Ms. Loretta brought over enough food to feed a whole army."

"No." She said, shaking her head and pulling out yet another family photo album. "I'm fine."

Estelle simply nodded and drifted off to another part of the house.

Alyssa sighed. Even though her stepmother had done everything she could to make her feel welcome, there was a part of her that believed Estelle wanted time alone so that she could truly grieve. But Alyssa struggled to give her that time because she needed the opposite.

She needed to be around anything and everything that reminded her of her father. Now more than ever, she regretted telling Tangie to go back home. She needed a firm shoulder to lean on. Estelle was too fragile.

Curling up in her father's favorite La-Z-Boy, she pored through the pages of the photo album. This one had a lot of pictures of the Hinton family. There were several pictures of her father and Roger Hinton bent over a chessboard.

Suddenly old memories filled her head. The men

would spend weeks playing the same game. One had even gone as long as a year. She didn't remember who won most of them, but she suspected that it was something like fifty-fifty.

Her father always said that you could tell a lot about a man by the way he played chess. The one thing he'd learned from Roger was that he was a man who never said *die*.

Alyssa chuckled to herself and flipped the page. She blinked, surprised to see images of her father on a large boat. She leaned in close and tried to make out the name on the side. *"Lady?"*

She frowned. Her father didn't own a boat. Maybe it belonged to Roger. She shrugged and flipped the page again only to learn that the boat apparently belonged to Sterling Hinton.

As she flipped through the pages, Sterling smiled back at her from nearly every corner—an almost silent guardian angel. Toward the back, more pictures of Quentin popped up and her smile vanished. She had so many mixed emotions when it came to him.

Still.

"I think I'm going to bed now," Estelle announced. "Do you need anything?"

"No, Estelle. Please don't worry about me. I'm doing fine."

Her stepmother nodded. "All right. Then I'll see you in the morning."

"Okay." Alyssa watched her turn and head off to bed. After hearing the click of the bedroom door, she sighed and then closed the photo album. For a long time, she just sat there, not really thinking of anything.

After a while, her ears picked up the solo ticking sound of the clock above the fireplace. In that moment, she felt like the loneliest woman in the world. For no reason at all, she uncurled from the chair and marched down to the guest room, but as she passed the master bedroom, she caught the sound of Estelle's soft sobs drifting through her door. She stopped and placed her hand on the door, but then continued on her way to the guest bedroom.

She quickly found her purse and searched through it until she saw what she was looking for: Sterling's business card.

Sterling was thrilled that he could be there for the Jansens this past week.

Truly he was.

But standing out in twenty-degree weather was probably *not* what the doctor would order. And as a result, he was suffering a relapse. A bad one. And there was no chicken noodle soup or half-spilled orange juice to get him through. This left him with only one option—to stay in his favorite spot in the bed and wait for his fever to break.

The phone rang.

"No. No. No. No," he groaned.

Maybe there's some soup involved? His hand shot out from under the cover. "Toni?"

There was a pause and then, "Um. No. It's Alyssa."

Sterling's eyes popped open. "Alyssa?" He climbed from under the blankets. "Is there something wrong?"

Another pause. "No. I, um…you know this is silly."

"No. No. It's fine." He removed the phone from his mouth, coughed and then returned it as though nothing had happened. "How are you holding up?"

"Not so good," she admitted. "My alarm clock never rang. I guess that means all of this is not a dream."

"No. I'm so sorry." A long silence stretched across the line, and Sterling strained to hear her soft breathing.

"I don't know what I'm going to do without him here," she said. "He was my rock, my anchor. Do you know that there wasn't a day that we didn't talk? No matter where I was in the world, he was my last call before going to bed." Alyssa sniffed. "Who am I going to call now?"

It was just on the tip of Sterling's tongue to suggest that she could call him, but it didn't sound appropriate even in his own head. "You can still talk to him. He'll always be watching over you."

"Yeah. Him and my mom."

Sterling closed his eyes and swore that he could hear her heart tearing into pieces. It wasn't too often he'd been thrown into this type of situation, and he prayed that his inadequacies weren't showing.

As it turned out, Alyssa did most of the talking. Sterling nestled down in his blankets and just enjoyed the soft cadence of her voice. It was really soothing. "When are you going to return home?" he asked.

"I don't know. Maybe in the next couple of days. Maybe tomorrow. I haven't decided. A part of me feels like just getting in the car and driving. Clear my head."

"I don't know. It's a long way to California. You meet a lot of weirdos on a trip like that."

She giggled.

"Haven't you ever seen that one movie *The Hitchhiker?*"

"I won't pick up just anyone."

"What about all those scary roadside motel movies?"

"I'm sensing a pattern. Are you going to warn me about the perils of driving on Friday the thirteenth or how not to do any babysitting on Halloween?"

"I'm not now."

She laughed and he couldn't help but join in. Of course, he had to hit the mute button to cover his subsequent coughing frenzy. But for the next few hours, they just talked and talked.

It was a good night.

Chapter 17

Alyssa slept like a baby.

When the sun's early-morning rays warmed her face, she stretched out on the bed with a soft smile curling her lips. After she opened her eyes and remembered where she was and the events of the past week that warm feeling that she had disappeared. She moved to get up and was startled when the cordless phone slipped from the crook of her neck.

She picked it up and placed it back against her ear. At the sound of soft, even snoring she asked, "Sterling?"

There was a low grumbling and then, "Yeah. Yeah. I'm still here."

Alyssa laughed. "Oh my God. I can't believe it. We both fell asleep on the phone."

"Uh, really?" He still sounded confused. "What time is it?"

She searched around and found a clock on the nightstand. "About eleven-thirty." She laughed again. "The whole morning is almost gone."

Sterling moaned again. "Who fell asleep first?"

She stretched again as she tried to think. "You know I honestly don't know."

"Then I guess that's a good thing. That means we both bored each other to sleep."

"Hey!"

"Just joking."

Alyssa shrugged. "Yeah, but it's kind of true." She paused. "Look. I really appreciate you being there for me last night. I feel a lot better. Thanks."

"Don't mention it." He coughed and the line went silent.

"Hello, Sterling. Are you still there?" She glanced at the phone, and then listened again. "Sterling."

Another cough. "Yeah. Yeah. I'm still here. I just hit the mute button for a minute."

His voice sounded odd. It was deeper and almost hoarse.

"Are you all right?" she asked.

"Fine. You know how it is in the morning." He coughed again.

She frowned but shook off the concern. "Well, I

guess I better let you go. I probably should check on Estelle and Jessica."

"All right."

"Again. Thanks for getting me through the night."

"Anytime. That's what friends are for."

Friends. Alyssa smiled. She and Sterling rarely saw each other, but it felt good to know that when they did, there was a strong bond of friendship. "Bye."

"Bye."

Still smiling, she disconnected the call and climbed out of bed. Truthfully, she didn't know what to make of a man who'd spend an entire night on the phone with her. Men didn't do that sort of thing. But in an odd way she was glad it was him and not Tangie. She just couldn't put her finger on why.

After a quick shower, Alyssa dressed and then wondered whether it was time to pack her bags and head for home. It really was getting to be about that time. She left the guest room and quickly discovered that she was the only one in the house.

On the refrigerator was a note: "Be back by one."

Alyssa glanced around and then made herself some coffee and grabbed a grapefruit for breakfast. As she sat at the kitchen table listening to the quiet house, she realized that it really was time to go back home. As much as she wanted it, this house wasn't going to fill the hole her father left inside her heart.

After she finished her breakfast, she returned to the guest room and started packing. By the time Estelle and Jessica returned, Alyssa had lugged her bags out to the rental car and was on the phone with the airlines. Because of the holiday season, her only option was to fly standby.

It would have to do.

"Ally! Ally!" Jessica hollered, running into the house. "Guess where we went."

Alyssa beamed a big smile at her little sister and opened her arms in time to catch her when she launched up into her lap. "I give up, where did you go?"

"We went to the mall, and we saw Santa Claus!"

"Oh really?" Alyssa widened her eyes in feigned surprise. "That sounds like fun!"

"It was." Jessica nodded. "You should have seen him. He's a reaaally big guy."

Alyssa laughed as her heart tightened. She remembered her father taking her numerous times to see Santa Claus when she was a little girl. Christmas was in a couple of weeks and it pained her to think of what the holidays would be like this year.

Estelle smiled from the bedroom doorway. "It was on the calendar to take her today. I figured it was best to keep up tradition."

Alyssa nodded. Life goes on. "So what did you ask Santa for?"

Jessica joyfully raced through her long laundry list—even the items she wanted to give *Daddy* when he woke up.

Meanwhile, Estelle's studious gaze took in the scene. "Are you leaving us?"

Alyssa's eyes dropped. "Yeah. I figured it was time."

Estelle didn't argue. "I think Jessica and I are going to visit my mother in Florida for Christmas," she said, frankly. "I just need…to get away."

Alyssa truly understood. "We'll get together next year."

"Absolutely. And every Christmas after that."

"Great."

"Momma, I'm hungry," Jessica complained.

"All right. C'mon. I'll fix you some lunch."

Alyssa quickly said her goodbyes and made her way out to the car. Once she was behind the wheel, she briefly entertained the notion of just driving all the way back to California. *It would definitely be an adventure.*

She started the car and glanced up at the house one last time before pulling out of the driveway. Once she hit the open road, she had every intention of going to the airport, but instead she headed out to Alpharetta to say goodbye to her friend.

Despite the stuffy head, the uncontrollable coughs and a temperature that just wouldn't break, Sterling still tried to convince himself that he was feeling much better. At least today he managed to cook his own soup. It was either prepare it himself or perish. He hit the shower, changed the bedding and then promptly crawled back into it.

If only this damn fever would break.

But there was something about his butt hitting the sheets that made his phone begin to ring. "Hello."

"Sterling?" Alyssa's now-familiar voice drifted over the line.

A smile instantly caressed Sterling's lips. "Hey, you."

"Hey. You'll never guess where I am."

What was with everyone wanting him to play a guessing game? "I give up. Where are you?"

"At your gate," she said.

He popped up. *"My gate?"*

"Yeah. Surprise!"

He didn't say anything.

"I—I hope this isn't a bad time. I was headed to the airport and I figured I'd drop by before I go."

Sterling sprang out of bed in a panic. His place was a wreck. "You're here *right now?*"

"Um, yeah. I…if it's not a good time, I understand."

"No. No. It's all right." He shuffled around his bedroom, trying to find something to put on. "Come right on in." He punched in the gate's code, hung up and transformed into a Tasmanian devil, whipping about the room as fast as he could. When he reached the stairs he nearly tumbled down them.

The living room wasn't too bad, the kitchen was a wreck and…did he have his shirt on backward?

No. Inside out.

No. Backward.

How in the hell did this damn thing go?

The doorbell rang.

"Damn it. Damn it. Damn it." As he raced to the

door, he saw that he had one blue sock and one black sock on. Why had he bothered with socks? He bent over and tried to pull them off, which resulted in him hopping on one leg and then the other. He ran his hand down his face and frowned at the sharp stubble.

Good Lord, why didn't I shave this morning?

The doorbell rang again.

"Coming!" He continued to hop his way to the door. It was too late to do anything else about his appearance. He just had to hope that he didn't scare her off. When he finally reached the front door, he drew a couple of deep breaths. Of course, his head was spinning now, but he'd think about that later.

He unlocked and opened the door. "Hey," he said with perhaps a bit too much enthusiasm.

She stepped back and blinked up at him.

Uh-oh. Something must be wrong.

"Um." Her gaze traveled over him. "Are you sure this isn't a bad time?"

Sterling glanced down and saw that he'd put his inside out *and* backward shirt over his pajama top and the latter was sticking out. And since when did he own striped pants. "No. Um, I just kind of threw this on."

"I gathered that." She laughed. "Can I come in?"

"Oh, sure." He stepped back. "Come on in."

Alyssa entered the house while Sterling gave himself a firm mental kick. At last he closed the door and turned to face her with a wide smile. Only he wobbled on his feet. "Sooo…hey!" he said awkwardly. "Welcome to my place."

"Thanks." She stood there smiling, not knowing what else to say.

"Well, why don't you come on in and sit down." He gestured her toward the living room.

Alyssa turned and walked, taking her time to assess the surroundings. "Nice place you got here."

"Thanks. I've only had the place for a year."

She nodded. "I remember Dad telling me when you moved from New York."

"Well, Jonas and I used to share a penthouse some years back."

"Yeah. I remember."

Sterling coughed.

"Did you decorate the place yourself?" she asked, taking in the classic black-and-white furnishings. Typical bachelor.

"No. I hired someone. Of course at the moment, I'm in between maid service, so please excuse any dust you might see."

She bobbed her head while the room filled with another awkward silence. What happened to that easy comfort they'd always had with each other?

Sterling coughed again. Only this time, he couldn't seem to stop.

Alyssa's expression collapsed in concern. "Are you sure that you're okay?" she asked. "You look… sick."

"No. I'm fine." He launched into more coughing.

Her eyebrows rose with her open disbelief.

Now his coughing turned into hacking.

"Sterling, you're sick as a dog," she admonished. "Why didn't you say something?" She rushed over to him and placed her hand against his forehead. "You're burning up." Alyssa quickly set her purse down and wrapped her arm around his waist. "C'mon. Let's get you in bed. I can't believe you."

"No. It's okay," he protested weakly.

"I'm not taking 'no' for an answer," she told him, leading him out of the living room. "Now which way?"

"Upstairs." He limped along, coughing the whole way.

It took some time, but she finally got him to his bedroom and then helped him tumble into his bed.

"I can't believe you didn't say anything," she fussed. "At least now that ridiculous outfit makes sense."

"Hey," he moaned. "This is the hottest trend."

"Now I know you're delirious."

"Humph. And you call yourself a fashion model." He lapsed into another coughing frenzy.

"Have you been taking anything?"

Sterling gestured to a nightstand that looked like a mini pharmacy. His headache was now a full-blown migraine, and his throat felt as if he'd spent the last twenty minutes chomping on sharp glass. In the distance he heard Alyssa rummaging around. In quick succession, he was handed pill after pill and capfuls of medicine.

And just when he was starting to feel better, his new wonderful nurse placed a cool compress against his head. *Now this is what I'm talking about.*

"Get some rest," she ordered. "I'll be right here when you wake up." She kissed his fevered brow.

That was all Sterling needed to hear before promptly falling asleep.

Chapter 18

Alyssa smiled down at the handsome giant nestled beneath the heavy blankets and bedspread. To her surprise, she actually liked taking care of him. It was the least she could do, given how he'd been there for her last night...and a few other times in her life. Being this close up, she took full advantage of really looking at Sterling as a man and not simply as...well, her old friend.

Sterling Hinton. Mr. No Nonsense. Mr. Independent.

In truth, this was the first time she'd ever known him to *need* help, to *need* somebody. She'd always viewed him as being such a strong man, a formidable man who had a secret soft side—but this vulnerable side was a different thing entirely. Was it so strange to be attracted to this vulnerable side of him?

Resigned that she would not be going home today after all, Alyssa returned to the living room and grabbed her cell phone and called Tangie. She reached her voice mail again and left another message. She went to the kitchen, saw the mess it was in and rolled up her sleeves and got busy. When she was through, she checked in on Sterling and saw that he'd kicked his way out of the blankets and his feet were dangling over the edge while his arms were wildly sprawled out over the bed.

Alyssa moved over to the bed and tucked his feet back in. She checked his temperature and frowned at how hot he still was. "Poor thing." Sighing, she glanced around to see if there was anything else she could do for him. There wasn't, but surely Sterling wouldn't mind if she gave herself a tour of the place.

And what a big place it was. Not as large as his parents' estate, but it was majestic and homey at the same time. It easily had eighteen-foot ceilings, including the upper floor, a two-story foyer, and hardwood floors throughout. She counted six bedrooms, each with its own bath, a huge wine cellar, theater room, exercise room and an impressive walnut gentleman's study. Not bad for a bachelor.

When Alyssa entered the study, she realized that it, like his bedroom, most closely reflected Sterling's personality. It was warm and inviting, yet erudite— just like its owner. Slowly she moved about and absorbed every detail, but it was the floor-to-ceiling bookcases that drew her like a magnet. Sure, there were a large number of law and economics books, but there was also a wide array of literary and popular fiction crowding the shelves.

She ran her finger along the hardback spines, seeking something she could delve into. She stopped at Chinua Achebe's *Things Fall Apart,* her father's favorite book. Alyssa smiled and pulled it off the shelf. When she cracked open the cover, she noticed the inscription:

> To Sterling,
> May this wonderful story enrich your life as much as it has enriched mine.
> Your faithful friend,
> Alfred.

Alyssa's eyes misted as she closed the cover and pressed the book up against her bosom.

In one corner, two huge leather chairs sat on opposite ends of a large walnut table with a beautiful marble chessboard in the center. Clearly he was in the middle of a game with someone. One quick glance at the pieces told her that the black king was just three moves from a checkmate.

She eased into one of the leather chairs to get ready for a long night's read.

Then there was a loud *thump.*

Her heart stopped. "Sterling?"

She strained to hear, but there was nothing. She

uncurled out of the chair and set down her book to go and investigate. The moment Alyssa stepped out into the hallway, she heard it again.

Thump.

Concerned, she rushed down the long hallway and made it back to the master bedroom. There, sitting on the edge of the bed sat Sterling. Head low, shoulders hunched.

"Is everything all right?" She rushed over to him. "What are you doing out of bed?"

He frowned up at her. There was no sign of recognition. "Cold. Needed to turn up the heat."

Was he kidding? It was like an oven in this room. "I'll take care of it for you," she assured him. "Now you get back into bed." Alyssa pulled back the blankets and directed him to return there.

Lacking the strength to argue, Sterling slowly rolled back, and she quickly pulled the covers over him.

"Thermostat. Thermostat," she mumbled as she roamed back through the house. It was like going on a scavenger hunt. She finally found it at the other end of the hallway. After fumbling with the digital controls, she returned to the bedroom. "The heat should kick in soon," she told him.

"Fire," he moaned.

Alyssa frowned and then glanced around. She eyed the fireplace across the room. She quickly opened the grate, and in a few seconds had a nice little fire going. Of course at this rate, they were going to be boiled alive.

"All right. I'll have you all fixed up here now." She returned to the bed and felt his forehead. He still had a fever, but he shivered beneath the blankets.

"I-it's cold," he complained.

He looked so childlike that her heart broke for him. Without a second thought, Alyssa kicked off her shoes and slid underneath the blankets.

Who knows? Maybe a little body heat was just what he needed.

Chapter 19

Sterling went from being cold to being warm all over. The drastic temperature change made him sigh in contentment while easing on a satisfied smile. The good feeling didn't stop there. Parts of his body began to tingle as if something was brushing against his chest, eyes, nose and even lips. Other parts of his body began to harden.

He snuggled up against this soft pillow in his arms. Plus this pillow smelled incredible. He drew in a deep breath and swore that he smelled a sultry blend of citrus, roses and even a hint of vanilla. Surely, he was imagining that.

Right?

Sterling nuzzled the pillow again and the persistent fragrance triggered his imagination or maybe it was a memory.

Maybe both.

In an instant he traveled back in time. He was walking across his parents' estate, heading to the solarium…where Alyssa Jansen waited. The music was clear as the air, while a sliver of moonlight cast the flowers and plants in a romantic glow.

"Quentin?" Alyssa's soft voice drifted from behind a tall plant. When she stepped out into view, it was like a star stepping out into the spotlight.

Sterling sucked in a small gasp. Her beauty seemed to grow every time he laid eyes on her. How was that possible?

"Oh, Sterling." She smiled awkwardly. "I thought you were someone else."

He smiled. "I kind of gathered that." He stepped forward, hating more than ever that he was the bearer of bad news. "I'm sorry to have disappointed you but, um…"

"He's not coming. Is he?"

Sterling drew in a deep breath and then slowly shook his head. "I'm sorry."

"I see."

After a long silence Sterling felt the need to fill it. "Something, um…came up."

She nodded absently, but at the same time, she looked so small. Was she embarrassed?

"He wanted me to send his apologies."

"Did he now? Or did your father send you?"

Sterling didn't know what to say. For a few seconds, the music just drifted between them.

"What do you have there?" She straightened her shoulders and stiffened her spine.

Sterling had forgotten about the champagne. "I, um, maybe we could share a drink."

Alyssa smiled. "You always were the nice one."

"And nice guys always finish last," he joked.

Her smile broadened with a hint of sympathy.

"So how about it?" he asked. "Want to share a drink with an old friend?"

"Are we?" Their gazes locked. "Friends?"

"I always thought so."

"Really?" she asked dubiously. "You don't look at me and see me as just a servant's daughter?"

"No." But he had hesitated.

Her smile faded. "I think I'll have that drink now." She reached for the bottle, and when her hand brushed his, there was this weird staticlike spark that caused his whole arm to tingle. Out of reflex, he stepped back.

"I'll open it," he said, covering his reaction. He handed her the glasses while he worked the bottle's cork.

Maybe it was the music or even the moonlight, but Sterling was suddenly nervous being alone with his...*friend.*

The cork popped and a small rush of champagne bubbled over the top.

"Whoa." He laughed.

A smiling Alyssa held up their glasses while he filled them. He placed the bottle down on a stone ledge and took his glass.

"So what should we drink to?" Alyssa asked. "My making a fool of myself?"

"Of course not," he admonished. "You're being too hard on yourself."

Sterling stared at her. Her dark gaze seemed to shimmer beneath the moonlight. "Why don't we drink to you?"

"Me?" Her eyebrows arched.

"Why not? I always make it a habit to drink to beautiful women." He stepped closer. "And you're by far the most beautiful woman here tonight." He took his time letting his gaze roam over her face.

Smiling, she clinked her glass against his. "Thank you." She sipped her champagne while the orchestra played, "Isn't It Romantic?"

"Care to dance?" Sterling asked, holding out his hand.

Alyssa giggled. "I never thought of you as much of a dancer."

"I'm not." He shrugged. "But I can rock back and forth pretty good."

"All right." She set her glass down and then glided into his open arms.

Sterling led her in a slow two-step while he hummed in tune. God, she felt so good in his arms. She was hard and firm yet soft and pliable at the same time. And her scent, that wonderful smell of soft citrus, rose petals and a hint of vanilla. She was completely seducing his senses. He couldn't stop himself from nuzzling his face deeper into the crook of her neck. Before he knew it, he was peppering kisses along the column of her neck and pulling her firmly up against his chest.

Alyssa sighed, her warm breath drifted across his ears, instantly giving him an erection. His lips then traveled across her collarbone and he could feel her quiver in his arms. "We shouldn't be doing this," he whispered.

Her answer was a near-orgasmic moan. She didn't stop him or push him away and that was all the encouragement he needed. His hands traveled down over her firm, round backside until he filled them greedily and squeezed.

His reward was another sultry moan. "God, you're beautiful." He nibbled on her ear while he now hiked her dress up inch by inch. "Do you know what you do to me every time I see you? Mmm?"

"N-No," Alyssa panted.

She sighed, pressing forward and jamming up against his erection, which he struggled to control. Every muscle in Sterling's body strained and tightened as he needed more and more of her.

Instead of unzipping the dress, Sterling quickly whipped it over her head and then gasped in surprise at the sight of her luscious curves in an exotic, red-laced bra and matching panties. The moonlight danced off her warm complexion, making her look more like an angel than any mere mortal.

Sterling pulled her back into his arms with a groan. "I want to make love to you," he rasped. "I *need* to make love to you. I'll go crazy if I don't."

Even in this fantasy, it was important to Sterling that Alyssa was a willing participant. It was as if there was some small voice in his head trying to tell him what they were doing was wrong, despite the fact Alyssa was a grown woman and despite that he'd known her for most of her young life.

"Tell me you want this," he panted. "Tell me you want *me*."

Alyssa was hot, bothered and confused. When she'd climbed into bed to offer Sterling her own body heat, she never thought—or even suspected the wild emotions that would come into play. The moment she'd huddled against him, she was instantly seduced by his quiet strength.

It should have felt weird lying in bed with him like this, but instead it felt like the most natural thing in the world. It was like she truly belonged locked against him. Then she began playing with fire, taking advantage of the fact that he was knocked out in NyQuil slumber. She thought it was harmless to run her hand across the wide span of his chest. Who would it hurt if she ran her finger along the outline of his closed eyelids, nose and lips?

She'd always known him to be handsome—all

the Hinton men were, but there was a quiet beauty about Sterling, too.

However, Alyssa forgot that for every action there's a reaction.

Her sleeping giant stirred and pulled her close as if she was his favorite pillow. Then he started nuzzling and caressing her. And it felt good. She figured if she lay still, neither stopping nor encouraging him, he would stop and fall back to sleep.

But then came the kisses.

His soft full lips against her neck and collarbone detonated unbelievable heat waves of pleasure that had her melting from the inside out.

"Do you know what you do to me every time I see you? Mmm?"

"N-No," Alyssa panted. Was this real? Was all this really happening? Maybe she was the one that was dreaming. *If so I don't ever want to wake up.*

"I want to make love to you," he rasped. "I *need* to make love you. I'll go crazy if I don't."

Hell, she was feeling the same way. She was so hot and wet that she wasn't about to stop whatever was about to happen.

Sterling pulled her top and she helped out by whipping it and her pants off, so that now she lay beneath him in only her red bra and panties.

"Tell me you want this," he panted. "Tell me you want *me.*"

She did want this—more than she could remember wanting anything. Her senses went haywire.

"Tell me," he insisted.

"Yes," she whimpered. "I want you, Sterling."

His lips rubbed against hers with a groan. He was like a starving man diving into a banquet. Her head spun like it was caught up in a tornado, while her nipples tightened and ached.

She rubbed the bands of his muscles as he shifted to hover above her. Giving in to her own frenzy, she tugged and pulled off his clothes. Naked, she drank in the sheer size and beauty of him. The moonlight made him look like an ebony god sent to her just for her seduction.

"I want you, Sterling," she repeated, trembling from the truth of her words.

A kind smile splayed at his lips before his head descended. This time the kiss was more tender and sweet, but just as dizzying. At the same time, Sterling glided a hand in between her legs. One finger slid easily into her warm, slick passage. She sighed and arched against his gentle invasion. It was no surprise the fierce beating of her hard clit matched that of her racing heart.

When he started stroking her, she whimpered and writhed beneath him. He slid in a second finger and then a third, spreading her wider and plunging deeper. Soon their kiss ended, but Sterling paid homage to her body as he inched over in the bed. Seconds later, his tongue danced around a puckered nipple. He teased its hardness and then gave it small bites that absolutely drove her wild.

But that was nothing compared to when he spread her wide and dove his tongue so deep that she came instantly. She bucked and hit her head on the headboard. That didn't matter. Before she could finish riding out her explosive orgasm, his tongue stroked and wiggled at the very heart of her core. A second and third orgasm left her gasping for air.

It was all too much. Too intense.

But Sterling just continued to work her body as if he had a secret copy of the owner's manual. After his tongue finished stroking her so intimately, he put a finishing coat of polish on her pulsing clit and set off yet another orgasm.

However, there was no rest for the limp and weary. Sterling climbed back up and shared her body's sweet taste with another soul-stirring kiss. The best part was when he slowly but deliciously slid his thick, long shaft in her wet, tight body.

She gasped against his lips when it sank deeper and deeper. *Good God. How big is he?*

Alyssa started to crawl up the bed, but his hands locked on to her hips and held her in place. Ecstasy jolted up her spine when Sterling was fully planted. She instantly curled her legs around his waist and her arms around his shoulders.

"Jesus, you're so tight," he panted.

"And you feel so good."

His hips moved.

Her body quaked.

The large bed thumped.

Alyssa had never felt anything so exquisite. Tears leaked from the corners of her eyes. For his every thrust, she concentrated on squeezing her inner muscles and rotating her hips in a small circle. She loved the sound of his groaning and moaning while he continued to kiss her senseless.

Another orgasm began to build. Alyssa wondered if she would be able to survive its intensity. She could sense changes in Sterling's body. His muscles flexed and tightened. She suspected that they were on the verge of coming at the same time.

"Don't stop…" she urged. "I'm…" She gasped and sparks blasted behind her closed lids as she convulsed with another orgasm.

Sterling clenched his jaw. Her slick heat squeezed and milked him like a vise. His low growl morphed into a mighty roar as his own orgasm hit with such force that his entire body shook—and for a long time.

Completely spent, he slumped over to the side and crashed against a pillow. "My God. You were wonderful."

"So were you," she said, panting.

For a few minutes, they sounded like two athletes who'd just completed a marathon. Sterling's arms wrapped back around her. He even nuzzled another kiss against her neck before he drifted back to sleep.

Sighing with unbelievable contentment, Alyssa followed him back to dreamland.

Chapter 20

For the first time in days, Sterling woke up finally feeling like his old self. Clear head, clear chest and miracle of miracles—no coughing. Drawing in a deep breath, he uncurled his tall frame and stretched as far as his muscles would allow him.

That is until he bumped into something—or rather someone. He jerked up and snatched back the top blanket. At first all he saw was arms and hair.

A woman? What was a woman doing in his bed?

He tried to replay the events of last night, but for the longest time, he was just drawing a blank. Since the woman's back was to him, he leaned forward, trying to get a good look at her face.

What he saw shocked the hell out of him.

Oh-My-God!

Sterling quickly scrambled backward out of the bed, so fast that he fell over the edge. He smacked the floor, but bounced back up to see if he'd awakened her.

What the hell was Alyssa Jansen doing in his bed? And why was she curled up so snug under him? He glanced down and saw that he was naked. "Oh sweet Jesus."

Think, Sterling. Think.

But he couldn't. He was still drawing a blank. Relax. Calm down, he said to himself over and over. A few deep breaths later, he did remember her dropping by—what, yesterday? He had gotten sick again and she demanded that he get in bed. Lots of medicine and…what? She jumped in bed with him? That didn't make a lick of sense.

I didn't do it. I didn't do it. I couldn't have done it. I wouldn't have done it. Would I?

Dangling from one of the bedposts was a lacy bra, and suddenly he remembered last night's dream. But it wasn't a dream.

Sterling's heart raced. He had screwed up.

A door slammed somewhere in the house and Quentin shouted out his name.

"Oh, hell," he whispered fiercely. *What was Quentin doing here?* "Of all the days for him to remember the security gate code."

The whole situation had the making of a bad *Three's Company* episode.

The usually unflappable Sterling Hinton raced around his bedroom like a chicken with its head cut off. He didn't know which way to go or what to do. How in the hell could he possibly explain *this* situation after the grief he'd given his little brother about his trying to pursue Alyssa in the first place?

I slept with Alyssa.

His first insane action was to run over to the bed and toss the covers over Alyssa's head—to hide her, of course.

"Sterling, bro. Are you still up here in bed?" Quentin's voice was growing closer. *He's coming up here.*

Alyssa stirred.

Sterling grabbed his pajama pants and put them on in record time. "You gotta stop him," he mumbled and then raced to the bedroom door. Good thing. Quentin was just reaching for the doorknob. "Hey." Sterling stepped out into the hallway and pulled the door closed. "What are you doing here?"

"Wow. You're up." Quentin beamed, and then glanced down at him. "You must be feeling better."

"Can't keep me down for long." Sterling wrapped an arm around Quentin's shoulders and started leading him away from the door. "So what are you doing here?" he asked again.

"What, I need a reason to drop by and see my *favorite* brother?" Q smiled and patted Sterling on the back.

Sterling cocked his head.

"All right. All right. So you're my *second* favorite brother. At least you're in the top two."

"Gee. Thanks. Now what do you want?"

"Well, I rushed over as soon as I heard about Alfred. Xavier and I just got back in town and received your message."

"I called your cell."

"Had it turned off. I was um…busy."

"I take it you took a woman up to the ski lodge with you?"

"I *always* take a woman with me. In fact, I usually don't leave home without one." He laughed at his own joke. "Anyway, that's not the point. Soon as I got the message I raced over here. How's Alfred's family holding up?"

Sterling knew that by *family* he meant Alyssa. "Fine. Well, about as well as could be expected."

"Alice taking this whole thing pretty hard?"

There was that damn pet name again. "Don't worry about her. I think she's going to be just fine."

"I sure would like to send her my condolences. You know, as an old friend and all."

Sterling clenched his jaw in annoyance, mainly because he knew the angle his brother was working, and there was little he could do about it. Quentin did have a right to be able to give his condolences, but there was no way he would ever just leave it at that.

"Do you think you could get me her number?"

Sterling stopped at the bottom of the stair and just stared at his brother.

"No funny stuff," Q lied. "Just an old friend wanting to reach out to her in her time of need."

So you can cozy up to her and seduce her. What the hell was he saying? The girl was in his bed right now.

"Let me get back to you on that," Sterling said, wrapping his arm back around his brother's shoulder and then leading him toward the door. "I'm sure I have her contact back at the office. I'll call you."

Quentin's eyes narrowed suspiciously. "Now why don't I believe that?"

"I don't know. Maybe for the same reason that I don't believe that you just want to offer your condolences. When you left here last week you told me that you were going to track her down and make her your next wife."

Q quirked up a smile. "You have a good memory."

"Thanks."

"But I still want the number. Despite what you may think, I liked Alfred. He was a good man. And I considered him a friend—Alice, too."

"It's Alyssa, damn it."

Quentin cocked his head.

"Fine. I'll get you the number," Sterling covered as he finally reached the front door.

"Hey, wait a minute. Are you trying to get rid of me?"

"Of course not." Sterling opened the door.

"Good." Quentin sidestepped him and headed toward the kitchen. "Then you won't mind if I go make myself some breakfast."

"Now?" Sterling rushed to block his path.

"People usually eat breakfast in the morning."

"What I mean is that now isn't a good time for me."

"Fine." Quentin sidestepped him again. "I won't fix *you* anything to eat."

There was a noise upstairs and both men froze.

"What was that?" Q asked.

"What was what?" Sterling attempted to play dumb.

"Is there somebody upstairs?"

"What? No," he lied.

"Sterling?" Alyssa called.

Quentin broke out into a smile. "Why you old dog. Up here playing like you're sick and you got a woman in your room. I should have known. I thought I saw an extra car out there."

Sterling's relief that Q hadn't recognized Alyssa's voice didn't last long. He still needed to get him out in case Alyssa decided to come downstairs. "That's right. I have company so get the hell out." He grabbed his brother by the arm and pulled him back toward the door.

"Damn. Is it like that now?"

"You got it."

"Damn. So this is how you act when you get some, huh?" He laughed as Sterling opened the front door. "Fine. Fine. I'll leave. Calm down. This must be serious if you're keeping her away from me."

"You can say that."

"So who is she?" Q stalled.

"Out."

"The girl's gotta have a name. She has a momma, doesn't she?"

"You don't know her."

"Maybe I do. I know *lots* of women."

"Is that supposed to make me feel better?"

"I guess not," Quentin chuckled. "Some things are best not to keep in the family."

"Sterling?" Alyssa called again.

"Sounds like somebody is impatient." Quentin elbowed him.

"Out."

At last his brother tossed up his hands. "I'm leaving." He stepped out of the house. "Just don't forget to—"

Sterling slammed the door in his face and turned around in time to see Alyssa approach the upstairs banister. She looked absolutely angelic with her tousled hair and his top bedsheet wrapped like a makeshift toga around her body.

"There you are," Alyssa croaked. "I wondered where you disappeared to," she said, rubbing her eyes. "How are you feeling?"

"Good. I feel much better," he said. Of course at this moment his heart was racing and his erection was hardening.

"Great." She nodded and coughed weakly. "Because now *I* don't feel so good."

Chapter 21

Sterling bounded up the stairs two at a time. He checked her forehead and found it just a little warm.

"I am so sorry," Sterling fussed, sweeping her up into his arms and carrying her back toward his bedroom. "This is all my fault."

Alyssa laughed at his overreaction. "Don't be silly. Put me down."

He ignored the request until he had her back in his room. "Hold on. Let me strip the bed and put new sheets on here." He stopped. "Of course I could just move you into another room."

"None of the other rooms have as big a bed as this."

Alyssa's breathtaking smile put a few more

inches on Sterling's erection. *What the hell is happening to me?*

"I gave myself a tour yesterday," she said. "I hope you don't mind."

"No, um. Not at all. *Mi casa es su casa.*"

She surprised him by leaning up on her toes and wrapping her arms around his neck. "By the way, last night was wonderful." She rubbed her nose against his and then gave him the softest and sweetest kiss he'd ever known.

When she drew back, Sterling could do no more than stare at her. Whatever small thread of hope he'd held that last night was just a dream dissolved. It really happened. He'd taken advantage of Alfred's little girl.

He was going to burn in hell for this.

"Is something wrong?" she asked innocently.

However, before he could answer, Alyssa erupted into a series of chest-racking coughs. Sterling frowned. "I don't like the sound of that."

She waved off his concern. "It's nothing. I'm sure after a hot shower and some breakfast, I'll be good as new."

The image of her in a shower caused him to step back and glance around. Unfortunately, his gaze zeroed in on the bed. *I want you, Sterling.* He trembled at the sudden memory.

"What is it? Is the shower not working or something?" she asked.

"Uh, no. I mean yes." He shook his head to clear

more images filtering through his mind. How was he going to navigate through this? He hesitated. "Alyssa," he began, shifting his gaze back to her.

"Yes." Her arms slid around his waist as she pressed her firm and curvaceous body up against him.

The way her eyes lit up, there was no doubt in his mind that she could feel her effect on him. He should put some distance between them, but damned if he had the strength or the will to do it. "A-about last night," he stammered.

"Um, hmm?" She nibbled on his bottom lip.

"Exactly…what happened?"

She stopped nibbling and leaned back to stare up at him. "What do you mean?"

He swallowed. "It's just that…it's a little…fuzzy."

Her expression twisted in confusion. "How fuzzy?"

Sterling sensed that he needed to tread lightly. "I mean I remember making love to you."

Her smile returned with a measure of relief.

"I just don't remember…how it all got started."

A blush crept into Alyssa's face. "Well, that might have been my fault."

Sterling blinked in surprise and then slumped with a slight relief. He was looking for anything to ease the heavy burden of guilt that was crashing in him.

"You were cold," she said simply. "I was just trying to warm you up."

Well that was awfully generous of you. "Let me get this straight, you made love to me because I was cold?"

"Okay no. That didn't come out right." She

laughed. "I climbed into bed to give you some body heat since you were shivering beneath the blankets. But then I guess, I got a little carried away when I started…you know." She shrugged.

"No. I don't know." His eyes narrowed. It was beginning to sound like she'd taken advantage of his weakened condition, but there was no guilt or even regret in her demeanor. "Well, I started snuggling against you, feeling how wide your chest was and running my finger along your face. You're very handsome."

"Thank you." He stared at her. "Then what happened?"

"Then you started snuggling with me. Smelling my hair and kissing my neck. And then you started asking me questions."

He frowned.

Alyssa's smile only grew wider. "You started asking me if I knew what I did to you. Then you said that if you didn't make love to me that you'd go crazy."

Sterling's guilt returned in full force.

"I have to admit, I felt the same way." She was back on her toes and kissing him again.

He tried to be immune but failed, especially when her soft tongue glided into his mouth and began mating with his own. He groaned and pulled her close. For such a small woman she was able to conquer his defenses handily and easily. Without any help from him, Alyssa's sheet slipped off her body and revealed her dangerous curves in all their glory.

How in the world had he mistaken any inch of her for being just a mere dream?

"What do you say that we take a long hot bath together?" she asked.

No suddenly disappeared from Sterling's vocabulary. Instead, he let her take him by the hand and led him toward his large bathroom and the huge Jacuzzi tub. It was evident in the very way that she walked that she was having fun teasing him. She switched and rolled her hips as she walked and when she bent over to turn on the water, she deliberately pushed her tush up high and then smiled back at him.

Yep. I'm definitely going to hell for this.

Alyssa smiled and stood up again. "If I didn't know any better I'd say you looked scared."

"This is just…quite an adjustment."

"I know," she said, beaming up at him. "But a good adjustment, right?" Her hands roamed over his chest. "I mean…who would have ever thought."

Her eyes shone as if she was playing with her favorite toy. Didn't she see the problems with this?

"You know what we need?" she asked.

"What's that?"

"Some bath salts and bubbles."

The answer made him laugh. "Sorry. I'm all out."

"Doesn't matter. We'll make do." She turned and stepped into the large tub.

Sterling's eyes went back to her incredible body. There was still a small part of him that couldn't believe this was all happening, and being a practical man, he tried to search for a right angle in this situation—a reasonable argument that justified what he was doing.

He couldn't find one.

"You getting in?"

He hesitated. Stepping in that tub meant removing his pajama pants. It meant getting naked…in front of Alyssa. *Alyssa.*

"I promise to scrub your back if you scrub mine." She settled down into the tub and leaned back so his gaze could take its fill.

The pants came off and he was stunned to watch her open approval of what she saw. How in the world did he get here? And why wasn't he turning around and running for his life?

He stepped into the tub.

His soul be damned.

Alyssa sat up and made room for him as he leaned over and shut off the water. After which, she glided into his arms and extracted another mind-blowing kiss. With sin so sweet he might never care if he got his soul back. There was something about the way their bodies fit that scared him. Even then his erection continued to rise despite the tub's warm water.

He wrestled with his emotions even when his hands were slipping and sliding over hips and waist. Why in hell did she have to feel so good?

"You're so tense," she accused, breaking their kiss and smiling down at him. "I think I know just the thing to relax you."

Before he could say or do anything, Alyssa rose

up to settle her knees on opposite sides of his hips and then eased effortlessly down on his thick shaft. At that moment every thought, troubled or otherwise, emptied out of his head.

"Oh that's better," she sighed, smiling. "You look a lot more relaxed now." She eased up and slid down again.

Was he ever.

She leaned in close to him and moaned against his ear. "Do you like how I take care of you, baby?"

"Oh God yes." His hands locked on her hips. She was so tight, but could still take his full length. She set a slow torturous pace while her nipples hardened like diamonds as they rocked against his chest. But suddenly he wanted them in his mouth and he leaned forward to do just that. He licked and kissed, and then sucked and caressed her firm, plump breasts. He then surprised her by locking his arm around her waist and standing up from the tub.

"Whoa," she giggled.

Determined to finally take control, Sterling turned her around so that she stood with her back to him and then bent her forward so that her hands were braced on the tub's edge. He then eased into her from behind, squeezing her high, firm tush and moaning out to God once again.

His strokes were just a little deeper and a little faster.

She gasped and even squealed whenever his shaft hit a particular sweet spot. The water sloshed in the tub while their bodies slapped against each other. As the pace quickened, she then took to moaning his name and begging him not to stop.

Alyssa had never had sex this hot. A part of her thought that last night had been more fantasy than anything else. But now she had confirmation that Sterling really knew how to work her body over.

Well.

In a million years she would have never guessed that the straitlaced, serious-all-the-time businessman could be such a beast in the sex department. She never expected that she would one day become addicted to him. She came alive under his touch, grew bold when she sensed that he was having regrets. She wasn't so naive that she hadn't known what all his stammering was about before she lured him into the bathtub.

Alyssa didn't want him to regret last night. Nor did she want him to view her as anything other than a grown woman who desired him. If she had to seduce him morning, noon and night, that was exactly what she would do. She wasn't a little girl anymore. She was a woman who knew exactly what and who she wanted.

And she wanted him.

Gasping, Alyssa felt her inner walls ripple and contract. Heat swelled just below her clit and she knew she was about to come at any second.

"Are you ready, baby?" Sterling was losing his rhythm, but he clearly didn't want to come without her. Even that act of kindness made her love him more.

"Yes-yes," she answered in a breathy, on-the-verge-of-coming way.

Sterling's hips transformed into a jackhammer and Alyssa held on for dear life. So far there had been no two orgasms alike with Sterling and this time was no different.

She gasped.

He growled.

They came.

An hour later, Sterling and Alyssa made their way to the kitchen. Sterling wore a pair of casual jeans and a T-shirt. Alyssa, who'd retrieved her luggage from her rental car, wore a pair of black jeans and a pink cotton top. "What do you say to pancakes?" he asked.

"Uh, no. Do you have any grapefruit or something light?" She rubbed her throat.

"Sore?"

She frowned. "Just a little."

"That's the beginning of the end," he warned. "Let me get you a throat lozenge." He raced off and returned with an armful of cold remedies.

Alyssa just lifted a brow at him.

"I say hit it with everything early." He placed them all on the counter.

She reached for a Halls and thanked him. "It's going to be all right. I very rarely get sick."

He laughed. "Yeah. That's what I said when I volunteered to babysit my niece and nephew a few weeks back."

She coughed again and frowned up at him.

"Don't say I didn't warn you."

"You could have warned me when I was at your front gate that you were contagious."

"You knew that I was contagious when you crawled into bed with me."

Alyssa walked over to him and slid her arms around his waist. "Are you kidding me? It was the best thing I ever did."

She offered up her lips and he leaned down to accept her kiss. Afterward, the nagging began again, but he was determined to ignore it…for now. "All righty." He clapped his hands. "What about those pancakes?"

"No pancakes. I'm on diet."

Sterling's expression twisted as he stole another look at her curves. "A diet for what?"

"Humph. You've forgotten what I do for a living. The camera picks up everything."

He shook his head. "Well, we're not taking pictures today. We're eating a big hearty breakfast. *Together.*"

As if championing his announcement, Alyssa's stomach growled. She stepped back and laughed in embarrassment.

"That makes it two against one." Sterling tossed her a wink.

"But—"

"End of discussion."

"Well, I see you're still bossy as ever."

"And you're stubborn. Now get the eggs and bacon out of the refrigerator."

"We're having bacon, too?"

"There will also be no complaining. Now go." He smacked her on the ass.

Alyssa stomped over to the fridge…but hid her smile.

Together they prepared themselves quite a feast: pancakes, eggs, bacon, sausages and buttered croissants. At the first taste of carbohydrates, Alyssa's taste buds rejoiced and went on sensory overload in an orgasmic moaning spree that was worthy of a porno star.

Sterling, uncomfortable but a bit turned on, got so carried away, he started popping blueberries into her mouth just to prolong the strange food foreplay.

Alyssa, however, was in heaven. Everything tasted so wonderful. Her body was awash with pleasure. She started laughing at herself when Sterling fed her by hand. This was gluttony at its best…but it was also fun. She needed a little fun after the week she had had.

If Tangie could just see her now.

Plus, she was really beginning to like the sound of Sterling's laughter. Its warm, rich sound had a way of wrapping around her and making her feel safe. She also liked the way his eyes danced—had his eyelashes always been that long? She couldn't remember. How was it that she never noticed he had two dimples on one cheek?

Out of all the years that she'd known him, she couldn't remember him ever laughing this much or appearing so relaxed. She was good for him.

After breakfast in the afternoon, Alyssa surprised him by asking if he was up for a game of chess.

"I never knew that you liked to play," he said, intrigued.

"What makes you think you know everything about me?"

He laughed. "That's a good point. I'm learning a lot about you I didn't know before." He turned thoughtful.

Alyssa eased out of her chair and into his lap. "They are all good things, right?"

His smile returned. "Right."

"Good answer." She wiggled her rump and slapped another kiss on him. "So are we on?"

"Why not?"

They rushed up to his library, but Sterling hesitated to reset the board.

"Who are you playing?" she asked.

"Alfred," he said softly.

She stopped, stared at the board.

"He was kicking my ass, too."

She laughed. "Maybe we should take a picture of the board.

He nodded and went and retrieved a camera. "I'll send you a copy."

"You better." She coughed.

Sterling looked at her.

"I'm fine. I'm fine," she insisted. "Let's play."

She curled up into one of the leather chairs while Sterling picked up a book. "Oh, I took that down last night. I was going to read it."

"Your father gave me this book," he said, smiling.

"It was his favorite."

"And one of mine," he said.

They glanced at each other.

"Ready to get your ass beat?" she challenged.

"Oooh. Trash talk. I'm sooo scared."

"You better be."

Chess is not a fast game and for the next few hours, the new lovers remained hunched over Sterling's beloved board engaged in mental combat. Alyssa could tell by the twinkle in his eyes and the lines of concentration in his forehead that Sterling was more than impressed.

What made the day fun were stories they continued to share about her father. Most of them were heartwarming, the others were downright hilarious.

"I really did enjoy growing up on your parents' estate," she confessed. "I have nothing but great memories."

"You mean when you were always chasing after my brother?" Sterling closed his eyes and mentally kicked himself.

"Who knew I was chasing the wrong brother?" she countered.

Sterling looked up and saw her heart shining in her eyes. As much as he had enjoyed the last couple of days, he couldn't help but feel his age around her. "Yeah. Who knew?"

As the day breezed by and evening encroached, Alyssa's cough grew worse.

Sterling checked her temperature and shook his head. "I think we better get you to bed."

"But the game," she croaked. Her voice was a raspy version of itself.

Sterling stood and plucked her out of her chair. "We can finish it some other time."

She started coughing again. Her entire body bounced in his arms. "But I *never* get sick."

"Welcome to the club."

Alyssa laid her head against his chest and sighed.

When he entered his bedroom, he made a beeline straight to the bed. Within seconds he had her all tucked in, snug as a bug.

"Okay. So I'm sick," she relented.

"It's about time you admit it."

She smiled, but then poked out her bottom lip.

"What is it?" he asked.

"I'm cold," she whined. "I think I'm going to need some body heat to warm me up."

He laughed. "Is that right?"

She nodded and pulled back the covers.

Sterling shook his head, but he climbed in anyway. "All right, but no funny stuff."

"No funny stuff." Alyssa snuggled close, but slid her hand down his pants. "But definitely some *fun* stuff."

Chapter 22

For the next week Sterling and Alyssa locked out the outside world and lost themselves in their own reality. After the first twenty-four hours, Alyssa's mild cold disappeared—a phenomena that she attributed to their extensive exercise. It turned out that sex does a body good.

The rest of the time she made sure to erase any and all doubts that she detected Sterling was having about their new relationship. To her, age was nothing but a number. For him, she suspected that it was a major problem. So she needed Sterling to think as little as possible. She just wanted them both to feel—to get lost in the moment. As the days passed and they shared laughter as well as so many tender moments,

Alyssa convinced herself that she was winning the war for Sterling's heart.

Their age difference be damned, which was why she decided that they spend this night making love before the fireplace. Cradled into her favorite sixty-nine position, Alyssa took hold of Sterling's rock-hard shaft and tilted it toward her watery mouth. Just barely holding back from devouring him whole, she first ran her tongue around the wide tip and then watched how the muscles in his legs jumped. At the same time, she could feel his strong hands spread her open a second before his warm tongue dipped inside for a taste. She undoubtedly drenched his mouth and chin with her body's thick honey.

She moaned and then rewarded him by sinking a few more inches of his shaft into her mouth and bobbing back up. Greedy for more, his hips strained upward. With a smile, she went back down and set an even pace. Meanwhile, Sterling continued to lick her glistening sweetness until Alyssa quivered and struggled to remain on her knees. In fact that was the game he played in his head. He wanted her to come so hard that she wouldn't be able to stay upright. Even though her mouth felt good, his own orgasm wasn't important. For Sterling, it was all about giving Alyssa what she needed.

She pushed back against his face, groaning as he devoured her. But it wasn't all in his control. Alyssa worked her own magic. His cock was stretched harder than he could ever remember. He doubled his efforts. She had to come before him.

Alyssa gasped in between head bobs, but she could already feel her back loosen while her flesh quivered against his open mouth. Finally she couldn't take it anymore and she had to allow his shaft to spring free from her mouth as she came unglued and collapsed against Sterling's muscled chest.

Minutes later, they curled themselves up in front of the fire. "You know, sooner or later we're going to have to leave this house," Sterling said as he lazily stroked her full breast. "Real life is waiting."

Alyssa sighed. "I like this life much better."

His low laughter rumbled against the curve of her neck. "It is nice." He kissed the back of her neck. "But we both have jobs to get back to. My office is blowing up my phone and your agent is calling all the time."

"Sounds like you're trying to get rid of me."

"Of course not." Another kiss. "I'm just saying that it's time to get back to the real world."

Alyssa twitched her nose at him. "Tangie has everything under control. Besides, it's New Year's." She rolled over onto her back and stared up at him. "I can't think of anyone else I'd rather bring the year in with."

He smiled. "I couldn't agree more."

The orange glow highlighted Sterling's beautiful chiseled features. At these quiet moments, Alyssa couldn't suppress the suspicion that she'd always loved this man somehow. Whether it was the quiet rescue of her when she was being towed away in the back of a limousine or getting her father to let her attend Jonas and Toni's wedding. There was a natural comfort between them—a natural flow of love that seemed to have always existed.

Plus, there was something about the way he looked at her that made her feel more beautiful than any high-fashion, celebrity photographer or any glossy magazine cover. This wasn't like the silly childhood crush she'd once had on Quentin. This was a woman's love. She didn't just want to spend her days and nights making love to him. She wanted to take care of him. She wanted a future with him. She wanted…everything.

As she snuggled closer, enveloping herself in his scent, she thought about last night when she woke in the middle of the night and stole a few minutes to watch him sleep. It scared her just how strong her feelings were for him. How could true love have been so close and her not recognize it?

"What are you thinking so hard about?" he asked, smiling.

"Us," she admitted.

Though he continued to smile, she caught doubt flicker across his features. "What about us?" His hand descended to brush across her flat belly.

Alyssa gently covered his hand with hers and waited until their gazes locked again. When they did, she confessed, "I'm happy about us."

More doubt crossed his features and forced steel into her spine to ask, "Aren't you?"

Instead of answering, Sterling asked his own

question. "Have you considered that what happened between us here this past week has just been lightning in a bottle—our paths crossing at a time when we were both vulnerable?"

Though she should have been prepared, the question threw her off guard. "Of course not."

Sterling continued down the same path, though his gaze shifted. "You just suffered a terrible loss, Alyssa."

"And what—I turned to you because I needed a father figure?" Her forced laugh held a note of sarcasm.

"Maybe."

"That's bullshit." She sat up while tears burned the backs of her eyes. "I made love to you because…because I was attracted to you. I knew exactly what I was doing."

Sterling remained calm and cool. "And when did this sudden attraction take place?" he challenged gently. "A week ago, a year ago—ten years ago?"

"Why are you doing this?" Alyssa's dread was slowly turning to anger.

"I'm just saying that maybe we really need to evaluate what's going on here." The strict, stiff, nononsense Sterling Hinton was back…and Alyssa wasn't too happy about that.

"Evaluating," she repeated, climbing up onto her feet and marching over to his discarded T-shirt. She jerked it on. "You know what your problem is, Sterling?"

"I'm sure you're about to tell me," he said, sitting up.

"You *evaluate* too much. You *think* too much."

"And that's wrong?"

"Yes!"

He chuckled. "And here I thought that I was just being honest with you."

"Why is it so hard for you to believe that I've fallen in love with you?" she challenged.

He exploded up off the floor. "Because up until a week ago you were *attracted* to Quentin!"

"That was back when I was a kid!"

"Really? Because you looked pretty damn grownup when you were waiting for him that night out in the solarium," he yelled.

Alyssa blinked in the face of his anger.

"You went there that night even though you *knew* that he was engaged," he accused. "Admit it. You loved Quentin your whole life."

"What are you—jealous?"

"You know what—just forget it. I should have never brought it up." He leaned down and snatched up the blanket and pillow they had sprawled out across the floor.

"Wait a minute, Sterling." She walked over and grabbed his arm. "Talk to me."

"Fine. If you think you can handle it," he said. "Why wouldn't I believe that you still have a thing for Quentin? What if he popped up here right now and said that he wanted you? Would you dump me for him?"

"What in the hell are you talking about?" She

released his arm and stared as if he'd lost his mind. "Where is this coming from?"

"Answer the question!"

"I'm not going to answer something that damn juvenile. You're talking crazy."

"Face it," he snapped. "I'm just your damn consolation prize." He stormed out of the living room. "I'm going to bed."

"Sterling?"

"Good night."

Astonished, Alyssa stood in the center of the living room, blinking after him. *What in the hell just happened?* She replayed the whole argument in her head and still couldn't come up with an answer. The whole thing was ridiculous. If Quentin wanted her? What kind of question was that?

If he couldn't understand the difference between a childhood crush and what was happening now, what was she supposed to do? Frowning, she walked over to the coffee table and poured herself a glass of wine. Maybe they just needed a few minutes to calm down.

She tilted up the glass and then downed the contents in one long gulp. After she reviewed the argument a third and then fourth time, she calmed down and saw the truth. Sterling *was* jealous.

Now she felt flattered.

Alyssa couldn't change the past, but she could reassure him about how she felt now. That was all that he was asking for. She laughed at herself. Of course. His ego just needed reassurance. She took a couple more sips of wine straight from the bottle and then went upstairs in search of her brooding lover.

She found him in the shower. Smiling, she opened the glass door without an invitation and then gave her man something he could feel.

At long last, Sterling returned to work. When he first strolled through the office building's glass doors, he garnered quite a few stares, not because it had been so long since anyone had seen him, but because he was whistling. By the time he reached the elevator, he was humming. When he reached his floor, he was singing.

Settling behind his desk, his reliable right-hand man, Dalton Walker, scurried in, pushing his Clark Kent–like glasses up his nose.

"Welcome back."

"Glad to be back."

Dalton nodded and smiled. "Nice little ditty you're singing there. Pick that up in the sick ward, did you?"

Sterling's smile only stretched wider. "Let's just say that I had one hell of a nurse."

Dalton's eyebrows spiked. "Lucky bastard."

"That I am." He glanced around his desk. "So what did I miss?"

"A lot. I'll have my assistant forward you updated reports," he said, heading back out the door in time for Sterling's assistant, Beverly Jones, to rush in. "I just forwarded you your messages. You had a few deliveries come in while you were gone. This one wasn't business related." She handed over a FedEx package. "It came a week ago."

"What is it?"

She shrugged. "Came from an attorney's office. Looks like someone left you something."

Sterling frowned.

"And I have your brother on line one."

"Which brother?"

"The annoying one."

Sterling rolled his eyes. "Tell him I'm not in."

"Too late. I already told him that you were here," she said, heading back out of his office. "I'm glad, too. He's been calling every day."

"Oh, joy."

"Glad to see that we're on the same page."

Sterling set the FedEx envelope down and picked up the waiting call. "Hey, Q. What's up?"

"You tell me," Q laughed. "You and your secret girlfriend been holed up for a long time. I was beginning to think that I needed to send the fire department to break you out of there."

"Thanks for the concern, bro."

"Yeah. Whatever. Oh, don't worry about giving me Alice's phone number."

"Oh?" This was a surprise. "Yeah. I tracked down Alfred's widow, Estelle, and got the number from her."

Sterling didn't like the sound of that.

"I left her a message so I'm just sitting and waiting. Wish me luck."

Sterling wasn't about to do any such thing. "Look, bro. I have to get going. I'll call you later."

"Yeah. All right. Maybe we'll hook up for drinks this week."

"Sounds good." Sterling rushed off the phone and then slumped back in his chair. What the hell was he doing? This whole thing had the potential to blow up in his face.

Big-time.

His gaze fell on the FedEx envelope and he picked it up. It was from an attorney's office. One he had never heard of before. He scanned the contents. It was from Alfred's attorney. Apparently, Alfred had forwarded a letter to him. He checked the FedEx package again and noticed another envelope in there. He hesitated for a moment and then opened it.

Dear Sterling,

If you're reading this letter then it's safe to assume that I'm no longer around and we haven't finished that last chess game. Consider yourself lucky, kid.

Sterling smiled.

I need a favor. I come to you because I've been racking my brain about who I can trust to do this. And then it just hit me. I'm going to need someone to look after Alyssa. Of course I know that she would say that she didn't need any looking after, but I know different. It's bad enough that she has already lost one parent and losing me may be particularly hard on her. Though it has been my wish that she and Estelle would grow close, I fear the constant distance made that pretty hard. She may not feel comfortable opening up to a near stranger. But you, I suspect she would trust a little more. I know that you're a busy man. I come to you as a friend. If you could just be there for her, be that shoulder for her cry on, I would appreciate it. And if it's at all possible, keep her away from your prowling brother. As much as I like Quentin, I fear the constant charmer would take advantage of the situation.

Thanks again.

Don't think of this as goodbye but as "I'll see you later."

Your friend,

Alfred.

Sterling folded the letter and then slumped his head into his hands. "What have I done?"

Chapter 23

When Alyssa returned to her Malibu home, she felt as if she'd been gone for ages. Tangie started talking her ears off the moment she picked her up from the airport. She wanted to know every detail about this new romance between her and Sterling, and she was none too pleased when Alyssa tried to keep a lot of the growing love story to herself. She wasn't trying to be coy or secretive. She just didn't want to jinx it.

The relationship was already going be difficult. Long-distance love affairs fail for a reason. Add to it the taboo of the age difference, her childhood fantasy for Sterling's brother and Sterling's annoying but constant need to always do the right thing, and suddenly this *new romance* was on thin ice.

"Fine. Then don't tell me." Tangie huffed.

"Forget that I'm your best friend and that we've always shared *everything*. What does a lifelong friendship have to do with anything nowadays?"

Alyssa rolled her eyes as she marched into her kitchen and popped open the refrigerator. She frowned at her bare shelves.

"I had the maid clean it out," Tangie said. "All that vegetable stuff doesn't have a long shelf life."

"I'll just order a pizza," Alyssa said, picking up the cordless.

"Pizza?" Tangie blinked and then stared her down. "Okay. That does it." She snatched the phone from Alyssa's hand. "Who are you and what have you done to my best friend?"

Alyssa laughed. "Nothing. I'm just a woman who loves carbs now." She grabbed the phone back. "I must have gained ten pounds since I've been gone," she confessed. "And I love every one of them."

Tangie just continued to stare. "You still haven't convinced me that you're not an impostor."

Alyssa sighed with a smile. "Not only have I had the best sex of my life with Sterling but I ate…and ate…and ate. We made huge breakfasts and ordered three-course meals from the best restaurants every night. I'm talking about pasta, creamy sauces and *meat*. Steak. Chicken. Sometimes even fried." Alyssa rolled her eyes. "I haven't eaten like that since I was a kid, trying out all Dad's recipes." A smile hooked her lips. "Maybe I should start cooking. Keep my father's legacy alive."

Tangie frowned. "Can you even cook?"

"I can do pancakes," she boasted. "Sterling taught me."

"I see." Tangie crossed her arms. "Let's go back to that part when you said you had the best sex of your life."

Alyssa's face became flushed with embarrassment. "You caught that, did you?"

"It's hard to get something like that by me."

Alyssa drew in a deep breath while her smile stretched from ear to ear, but in the end she couldn't hold back. "It was incredible," she confessed. "Never in my life has a man just turned me out like that. It was incredible. It was fantastic. It was…beautiful." She set the phone down and grabbed Tangie's hands. "I love him, Tangie. I've been playing every memory I have and I don't know why I didn't see it before. He has always been protective, kind and patient with me."

"And Quentin?"

Alyssa waved off the question. "I haven't thought about Quentin in years. He was just a childhood crush. Puppy love."

"And Sterling is the real thing?" Tangie asked dubiously.

"Yes," she answered without hesitation. "He's my heart. I really want this to work."

To her surprise, her words failed to erase the doubt from her friend's face.

"What?"

Tangie shrugged. "Nothing."

"You're a lousy liar." Alyssa crossed her arms and prepared for the worst. "Out with it."

"Well…it all just seems soooo…convenient."

Alyssa's defenses flared. "What do you mean?"

"Look. It's cool if you're just trying to get your groove back. I'm with you on that. But…true love?" Tangie gave her a halfhearted shrug. "I don't know."

"See. I knew I should have just kept my mouth shut."

"C'mon, Ally." Tangie cocked her head. "You raced home because of a family tragedy and you wind up in the arms of a handsome…father figure."

Alyssa went still.

Tangie continued gently. "I mean. You were in a vulnerable state, right?"

"Vulnerable?"

"Yeah…and Sterling was a good friend of your father's. He was able to share and commiserate. He offered comfort."

"So fucking him was my way of saying what— thank you? Is that it?" Alyssa snapped.

Now Tangie became defensive. "I didn't say that."

"You might as well have," she said angrily. "I'm telling you it wasn't like that. Sterling and I connected. It wasn't pity sex."

"Okay. Okay. I take it back." Tangie tossed up her hands. "I didn't mean any harm."

But the harm had been done all the same. Mainly because Tangie's words sounded so much like Sterling's. Why was everyone determined to tell her how she felt? She shook her head and tried to erase the troubling thoughts.

But they were there to stay.

"C'mon. Let's go ahead and order that pizza," Tangie said. Clearly, she was trying to make up for bursting Alyssa's bubble.

Why didn't I just keep my mouth shut? "You go ahead and order, I'm going to go upstairs and change out of these clothes," Alyssa said, inching out of the kitchen. She needed some space and distance from her best friend right now.

"Ally, I didn't mean—"

"It's all right. I'll be back in a minute." She left her friend standing in the kitchen while mentally cursing her out. By the time she reached her room, her tears had blurred her vision. Needing to calm down, she whipped out her cell phone and dialed Sterling's office. Maybe hearing his voice was all she needed.

Unfortunately, she reached his robotic voice mail instead.

"Hey, Sterling. It's Alyssa. I just wanted to let you know I made it back home okay. I miss you already. I wanted to hear your voice. Give me a call when you receive this message. Love you. Bye." She hung up. Everything was going to be all right. She didn't have to prove anything to Tangie. What she felt was real. All she needed was to hear from Sterling.

But two days later, he still hadn't called back.

Alyssa called every number she had and left

multiple messages. She even went through the stage where she feared that he'd been in a bad accident or something. She called hospitals and clinics. She even called his parents' estate. Beatrice had heard nothing about any family accident or death. She thought about returning Quentin's call but couldn't shake the feeling that it would be the wrong thing to do.

Finally the truth was staring her in the face. Sterling was fine. He just wasn't returning her calls.

Still, she waited.

And waited.

And waited.

On the seventh day, she left a final message on his home answer machine:

"Sterling, this is Alyssa. By now I'm sure that you've received all of my messages." She drew a deep breath. *"You know you could have just told me to fuck off. I expected you to be more mature than this. Don't worry. I get it. You don't have to worry about me bothering you anymore. So have a nice life, asshole."*

Alyssa slammed the phone down and willed herself not to cry. Screw him. She hoped he rotted in hell.

Sterling replayed Alyssa's message and poured himself a drink. As he listened to the anger and bitterness in her voice, he tried to convince himself for the millionth time that he was doing the right thing.

No matter how much it hurt.

Why settle for one Hinton
when you can have two?

Chapter 24

Now...

Xavier frowned as he stroked his chin and tried to keep up. "So if Sterling and Alyssa broke things off, what's the problem? She was a free woman."

Quentin chuckled. "You obviously don't know women very well."

Xavier's gaze narrowed. "I wouldn't go that far. I've been in a relationship a time or two. Can't say that the serious stuff is my cup of tea, though."

"Take my advice and keep it that way."

They shared a brief laugh.

"Seriously, though," Xavier said. "If she and your brother broke up...?"

"Have you ever known a woman to say what she means and mean what she says?"

Xavier thought it over. "Can't say that I have."

"There you go."

"Sooo…Alyssa and Sterling broke up, but she didn't stop having feelings for him."

Quentin smiled and cocked an imaginary gun at him. "Bull's-eye. Now you're catching on. Only thing is, I entered the picture and didn't know the rules had changed…or that there were more than two players."

"I hate when that happens," Xavier commiserated.

"That makes two of us. I thought I was capitalizing on a childhood crush. I didn't know I was dealing with a woman still in love…."

Chapter 25

Last year...

The launch of Jansen Inc. became one of the most hectic times in Alyssa's life. Officially a retired super-model, she still had one of the top-selling fragrances in the U.S. and in England. Now she could officially add fashion designer to her résumé. Her first fall line was picked up by major department stores.

To celebrate, Tangie had planned a fabulous party in Manhattan. It was complete with red carpet and paparazzi. Tangie and her publicist kept calling it the hottest event of the year. Alyssa just called it more work—which it was.

Smiling, shaking hands and air-kissing while navigating through the fashion industry haters was a full-time job. At least it was shaping up to be quite a success. Everyone who was anyone showed up. The music was pumping, everyone was laughing and having a good time—everyone except the star of the party.

"Will you relax and loosen up?" Tangie shouted above the music. "You're supposed to be having a good time."

"I didn't get that memo," Alyssa said, reaching the bartender and thanking him for her third cocktail. "I think I would have been more productive if I'd stayed home and gone over Margie's sketches."

"Work, work, work. I swear that's all you do nowadays."

"It's the only thing that keeps me sane," she admitted.

"All work and no play make Alyssa a very dull woman." Tangie shook her hips. "Loosen up. You used to know how to do that."

I used to know how to do a lot of things, Alyssa thought, *but it all seems so long ago.*

"C'mon. There're a lot of single men in here tonight."

Alyssa rolled her eyes. "Well keep them away from me. The last thing I need in my life right now is a man."

"Ally," Tangie whined. "It's time that you jumped back into the dating pool. That whole Sterling fiasco was almost two years ago. Surely it's time."

"What makes you think that I haven't?"

"You mean other than the fact that you don't date

and you stay home most weekends, curling up with that damn dog."

"Hey, me and Doggie are just fine."

"I still can't believe that you named a dog Doggie."

"It suits him."

"Ms. Jansen!"

The women turned and were immediately drawn into a business conversation with a French buyer. Then Alyssa was congratulated by another string of models, actors and actresses.

More work.

"Everything's looking good," Tangie bubbled. "C'mon, be happy."

"I *am* happy." Just then Lil Jon's latest hit blasted through the club's speakers and Alyssa threw her hands up and started swinging her hips. And to shut Tangie up for good, Alyssa climbed up onto the bar and really got her groove on. Everyone went wild and cheered her on.

It felt pretty good.

A few more partygoers climbed onto the bar with her, others jumped on top of tables. After a few songs, Alyssa finally descended, still getting into the party mood.

"My, my, my. If I hadn't seen it with my eyes I don't think I would have ever believed it."

The familiar voice stopped her cold. When she turned around, her spirits dipped in disappointment. "Oh… Quentin."

"Hello, Alice." He strolled up. His bold gaze

roamed over her. "You're looking beautiful as ever. It's no wonder why half the women here are jealous."

Her lips curled. "I see that you're still quite the charmer."

"Guilty, but please don't hold it against me."

"Now why would I do that?"

Quentin shrugged one shoulder. "Oh, I don't know. You may be holding past grievances. It's the only reason I can think of why you never returned my calls."

"Sorry about that," she said. "I guess I've been a little busy."

Q nodded and glanced around the place. "I'd say that's an understatement. Congratulations. Looks like you're well on your way to moguldom."

"And you?" she countered. "Are you still searching for your calling?"

Quentin grinned.

"Or are you still marrying for mergers?"

Quentin cocked his brow. "Ahh. So you are still sore at me? I knew it."

"Hardly." She lifted her chin. "I've just moved on, that's all." She made sure that she kept her eyes leveled so that he caught her meaning. But judging by the twinkle in his eyes, she knew he just saw it as a challenge.

"How about we grab a booth and play catch-up for a while?"

"I don't know." She hesitated. "I'm sort of the woman of the hour."

"Then how about we get together for drinks tomorrow?"

Again, she hesitated.

Quentin cocked his head and gave his best puppy dog expression. "For old times' sake?"

She wavered and then, like most women, gave in to Quentin's charm. "You have yourself a deal."

Quentin couldn't believe his luck. After years of praying for a second chance with Alice, the opportunity had at long last presented itself at a party he almost didn't attend. He didn't know how it was possible, but she was even more beautiful than he remembered. After she left him in the center of the club to go network and dance around with her friends, Q's gaze followed her every move.

Don't screw this up.

The thought only added more pressure. When had he not screwed up? Screwing up was his specialty.

"There you are." Xavier pushed his way through the dancing crowd. "Man, you gotta try this drink." His cousin handed over a bubbling concoction that looked straight out of Dr. Jekyll's lab.

Quentin frowned. "I think I'll pass."

"Girls," Xavier said, glancing over his shoulder. "He says that he's not interested."

Out of nowhere, a sexy set of identical twins appeared at Xavier's side. The women wore dresses that left very little to the imagination and could easily earn them a ticket for indecent exposure if they stepped outside of the club.

"I take it that you see something you like," Xavier said with a wolfish grin.

Quentin took the drink.

"Your cousin's cute," the arm candy on Xavier's right side announced specifically for Quentin's benefit.

"Yeah. I say we ask him to join us for our own party," the left arm candy said.

Xavier's eyebrows stretched high in question above his Gucci shades.

Q caught sight of Alyssa from the corners of his eyes. His chest tightened whenever she smiled.

Xavier cleared his throat.

Quentin's attention jumped back to his cousin and then swung between The Hard-on Twins. "Sorry, man. I'm going to have to sit this one out."

The women pouted, poking out their bottom lips.

"Are you all right, cuz?" Xavier asked. His expression collapsed in confusion.

"Yeah. Yeah. I'm cool." He started to inch away from temptation. He didn't want the twin's gravity-defying tits to start clouding his judgment—which wasn't a hard thing to do. "I'm just going to hook up with you later," he shouted.

"All right," Xavier said. He shrugged as his grin spread wider. "It just means more for me."

Q gave him the thumbs-up. "Don't hurt yourself." He turned and made his way across the club. He even managed to find a free table where he sat down and continued to watch his Alice flitter about the room. He really had been a fool to let her get away.

He wouldn't make the same mistake twice, he vowed.

What he needed now…was a plan.

Chapter 26

"This is an intervention," Jonas announced.

Sterling frowned and glanced up from his piles of paperwork. "Come again?"

Toni stood up from her chair and moved next to her husband. "We're only doing this because we love you," she said. "But we think you have a serious problem."

Sterling was still lost. "And that would be…?"

"You work too much," they said in unison.

If it wasn't for their stern expressions and their serious tone, Sterling would have burst out laughing. Instead, he pushed away from his desk and leaned back in his chair. "I see."

"I don't think you do," Toni said. "You've always put in long hours. We know that, but in the past year you've taken things to a whole new level. Beverly says that you work seventeen hours a day, seven days a week."

"So my assistant is behind all this?"

"She's worried about you." Toni looked to her husband. "We all are."

Sterling calmly braided his fingers. "Look. I really appreciate the concern. Really," he stressed. "But as you see I'm fine. The company is growing, my stockholders are happy and Beverly wasn't complaining when she saw her bonus check a couple of months ago."

Jonas shook his head. "Sterling, man. You know I understand the thrill of closing a big deal, but there are some things that are more important in life. You need to get out and meet people."

"I meet people all the time."

"I mean…women. The kind of women you date, not hold a conference call with, or go over spreadsheets and financial statements with. Are you trying to become a monk or something? I mean, it's okay if you are," he added.

Toni bobbed her head. "Yeah. We'll love you just the same."

Sterling couldn't suppress his laughter any longer. "That's very understanding of the both of you. But I'm not trying to become a monk."

Jonas's shoulders slumped in relief. "Then what's the deal?"

"Does this still have anything to do with that mystery woman you dated a while back?"

Sterling's smile vanished.

Toni trodded lightly. "Q said that he'd dropped in when you were uh—"

"This discussion is over. I have to get back to work." Sterling picked up his pen and shuffled through his papers.

"Look. Obviously I hit a nerve," Toni said. "But we're just trying to help. The family misses you."

"Good Lord, Toni. It's not like I've died or something." Sterling shifted in his chair as he grew agitated.

"It feels that way," she replied. "What's this about you not coming to Roger's seventieth birthday party?"

"I have a business meeting in London," he explained. "I'm sending him a gift."

"Bring the gift *with* you when you go to the party."

Sterling tossed down the pen and then glared at them. They were prepared for this popular power move of his and met his intense glare with their own. In the end the silence was too much for Sterling. His hands shot up in surrender. "All right. All right. I'll go. Are you happy?"

"Yes!" They broke out in wide smiles.

"And make sure that you clear your calendar for the whole weekend. Your mother planned something for each evening."

Sterling huffed. "Of course she has."

They stood there beaming.

"Fine. Anything to get you two out of my office." Proud of their successful campaigning, Toni rushed around Sterling's desk and planted a kiss against his cheek. "You won't regret it. I promise."

He doubted that. "Okay. *Now* will you two leave?"

Jonas took hold of his wife and tossed him a wink. "See you next weekend."

Can't wait. Sterling watched them as they filed out of his office. When it was safe, he drew in a deep breath and exhaled it slowly. Despite his agreeing to attend this weekend-long celebration, his brain was already searching for a way to get out of it. Maybe he could fake a business emergency? He shook his head. Chances were that his assistant would rat him out. The traitor.

He could always fake an illness. Sterling went still, thinking about the last time he'd been sick and how Alyssa's offer of body heat had at last broken his fever.

"Stop that," he ordered himself. For the past year he'd worked too hard to lock those memories away. He'd even gone so far as to sell that damn house so that every time he took a bath, shower or even sat in front of the fireplace he wouldn't be overwhelmed by erotic memories.

Once in his new place, he then decided he needed to get rid of some of the furniture. He said goodbye to his big four-poster bed, his favorite leather chairs, a couple of ottomans and some exercise equipment. The only thing he hadn't done was perform an exorcism—and for a while there, he gave it serious consideration.

He couldn't get rid of the chessboard. The one game they ever played still waited for their next move. Clearly, she'd learned the game well. He was just two moves from being checkmated. The board felt a lot like his life. Despite all the work he'd put into forgetting her, it could all go to hell if she ever walked back into his life.

Sterling leaned back in his chair and opened the top drawer of his desk. He removed and unfolded Alfred's letter.

> I come to you as a friend. If you could just be there for her, be that shoulder for her cry on, I would appreciate it. And if it's at all possible keep her away from your prowling brother. As much as I like Quentin, I fear the constant charmer would take advantage of the situation.

No matter how many times Sterling read the letter, his disappointment in himself only deepened. What kind of friend couldn't do this *one* simple favor? How had he allowed himself to be cast in the same role as Quentin? "Sorry, Alfred, but the best thing I can do for Alyssa is to stay the hell away from her."

That was the only promise he planned to keep.

Kitty Hinton lived under the pretense that she didn't like sticking her nose where it didn't belong. But this was different. Desperate times called for desperate measures. As much as she loved Jonas and Toni for giving her two beautiful grandbabies, she wanted more. Knowing her sons as well as she did, her best bet was Sterling.

And she had the perfect woman for him.

"So you're sure that he's coming?" she asked Toni over the phone for the third time.

"It wasn't easy," Toni admitted. "I had to coerce my husband to play along, but I think it worked."

"He could still fake some business emergency or an illness."

"Well, we can't club him on the back of the head and drag him there," Toni reasoned.

"Why not?"

Toni laughed. "All I can tell you is I fulfilled my part of the arrangement. Are you sure that he's going to like this Sierra woman?"

"Oh yes," Kitty boasted. "She's beautiful, smart and a real outdoorswoman. She loves all that hiking and biking crap that Sterling does. I can't wait for you to meet her."

"I can't wait for Sterling to meet her," Toni said. "After seeing him today, I'm convinced more than ever that he's struggling over a broken heart. He won't talk about her. But whoever it was, really worked a number on him."

Kitty smiled. "Then we'll just have to fix that. Won't we?"

"I don't know, Quentin." Alyssa hedged as she sipped her Starbucks coffee. "I'd feel awkward going to your father's seventieth birthday party. I haven't been back to South Carolina since…since…"

"I remember." Quentin smiled and leaned forward

in his wrought iron chair. His smile and charm were working overtime. "I also remember you being one hell of a swimmer...and kisser."

Alyssa shook her head. "You don't give up, do you?"

"What? I'm just strolling down memory lane with you." He shrugged. "No harm in that, right?"

"We agreed to just be friends," she stressed. "It makes things awkward if I'm constantly fending you off." She broke her biscotti in half and fed it to Doggie, who sat heeled patiently by her leg.

"All right, we'll play things your way," Quentin said. "I still think you should come to Dad's birthday party. If for no other reason than to be my moral support."

"You and your dad still not getting along?"

"You'd think he'd be off my back now that I've started my own business."

"With your cousin, Xavier, right?"

"Yeah. The Dollhouse. It's a Gentleman's Club. We have one here in L.A., one in Atlanta and in New York."

"Well, good for you. You found something you liked and turned it into a business."

He nodded. "It took me long enough. But I'm my own man now."

Each time she laughed, Quentin's ray of hope of turning this friendship pact around broadened. He reached for her hand. "Come to the party. Dad would be thrilled to see you again. You know they consider you to be part of the family."

Still she hesitated.

"Surely your company can spare you for a weekend. All work and no play makes Alice a dull girl."

She laughed. "You still call me that."

"Old habits are hard to break. Come to the party."

Her gaze dropped to her coffee. "Will Sterling be there?"

"Everyone is going to be there," he chuckled. "Of course momma is pulling double duty and is using the opportunity to fix Sterling up on a blind date."

"Oh?" Alyssa suddenly became fascinated with petting her dog. "He's still a bachelor then?"

"Married to his work. As always." He sipped his own coffee and then cocked a smile. "Actually, I thought he'd finally found someone a while back. Sterling doesn't talk much about his love life. Now, not at all. It's all very…strange. I'm guessing whoever this chick was really did a number on him. I've never seen him so miserable."

Alyssa frowned and for a brief moment, Quentin thought he saw her eyes gloss over.

"Hey, now. I didn't mean to ruin the mood by giving you the 4-1-1 on my brother's love life." He laughed. "Sterling is a big boy. I'm sure he'll do better deflecting my parents' meddling. If not, the worst thing that could happen is that he'll end up marrying someone he doesn't love."

Alyssa's gaze shot up.

"So what do you say? Will you come to the party?"

Chapter 27

The minute Sterling returned to his parents' estate, he knew that something was up. His mother was the first one to greet him. She was too bubbly and animated by half.

"Oh, sweetheart. You made it." She leaned up and kissed each side of his face. Billy Dee Williams *the fourth* barked his greeting.

He forced a smile. "I couldn't miss Dad's big day." *Because none of you were going to let me.*

"Your father is going to be so happy to see you when he gets here." She patted his arm. "Set your bags down and let Antonio carry them up to your room."

"It's okay. I can—"

"Come. Come. I want you to see the decorations

and tell me what you think." She gave him no time to argue. She turned on her heel and marched through the house and then out the back door.

As Sterling followed, he tossed an occasional hello and friendly wink to his parents' longtime employees, who were busy cleaning and scrubbing in preparation for the long weekend. Outside, a couple of party planners ran around an army of workers. From what he could tell, it looked as though his mother was going to do a twenties and thirties theme, complete with a speakeasy bar, a section for a big band and he even saw Prohibition "bathtub gin."

"It looks like it's going to be one heck of a party," Sterling said, looking around.

"You think he'll like it?" she asked.

"He'll love it," he reassured. From the corners of his eyes, he spotted a small group of women on the patio. "You already have company?"

"Oh, yes. Come." She grabbed one of his hands. "I want you to say hello to everyone."

Sterling allowed his mother to lead him to the patio, where a group of friends sipped merrily from colorful glasses. "Hello, ladies."

"Hello, Sterling," they answered in chorus.

"Looks like you ladies have already started your own party."

"It's never too early to start," Ms. Nelson said.

The women held up their glasses for a quick toast.

Laughing, Sterling started to make his excuses when he noticed a new face. A younger face.

"Oh. Where are my manners?" His momma gasped and Billy Dee Williams barked. "Sterling, this is Sierra Edwards. Barbara Anne's daughter. She came up to visit her mother this week and I invited her to the party."

And there it was, Sterling realized. He had stepped into a perfectly laid trap. "Nice to meet you." Sterling smiled kindly at the pecan-brown beauty. Her sparkling eyes conveyed a sharp intelligence.

"It's a pleasure to meet you, too," she said in a soft honeyed voice. "I can't wait for the party. It looks like it's going to be fun."

"It will be," Kitty piped up. "Make sure you reserve a dance for Sterling here. With so many couples attending, I don't want the single people to feel left out."

Of course not. Sterling held on to his smile even though he felt as if he could easily chew through nails. He didn't want this. He didn't need this. However, there was no point in causing a scene or embarrassing his mother in front of her friends by storming off.

He was also pretty sure that Sierra was as much a pawn in this parental scheme as he was. "In that case, I would be thrilled to be Ms. Edwards escort for the evening, if she'd like."

His mother's face lit up.

"I'd like that very much."

Tangie and Alyssa sat parked at the LAX airport, watching people rush around with everything from luggage to children. After ten minutes of silence, Tangie turned toward her friend. "Are you sure you want to do this?" She folded her arms. "You're really playing with fire with this one."

"I know," Alyssa said solemnly.

"I mean you're going to this thing with one brother you used to like in order to go see the other brother you—what? What exactly are you hoping to get out of this?"

"Closure." It was the only real answer she had. It had been eighteen months of trying to forget the best week of her life and it simply wasn't working. It hadn't helped to have Quentin back in her life. At every turn she couldn't stop comparing the two brothers. While Q was playful and charming, Sterling was stern and mature. Quentin didn't waste a moment telling her how beautiful she was but it was Sterling that had made her *feel* beautiful.

Alyssa drew a deep breath while she struggled to explain her chaotic emotions, but she couldn't.

Tangie sighed and shook her head. "I owe you an apology."

Alyssa frowned. "For what?"

"For what I said to you when you came back from Georgia that time and for accusing you of just looking for a father figure. I should have been more supportive."

"Forget it." Alyssa waved off the apology. "You were just being honest. I *was* vulnerable then…but it didn't mean that what happened between Sterling and I was a mistake." She turned away and gazed back out of the window. "Clearly he thought it was."

"What if he still thinks that? What are you going to do then?"

Alyssa shrugged as tears burned her eyes. "I don't know."

"What about Quentin?"

"We're just friends," Alyssa said. "I made that clear."

"I don't know." Tangela shook her head. "He doesn't act like he just wants to be your friend. Morning walks, coffee at Starbucks and flowers just because? This has all the makings of a man in hot pursuit. Plus, what is Sterling going to think if you show up on Quentin's arm?"

"He probably won't care."

"Are you kidding? The man slept with you. He's going to care." Tangie cocked her head. "Or is that what you're counting on?"

Roger Hinton's seventieth birthday party was in full swing. As the big band blasted the hot jazz tunes, flapper dresses flapped and an army of zoot suits tried to play it cool on the dance floor. Roger, Kitty and Billy Dee Williams greeted everyone with boisterous laughs, wide smiles and long-winded stories.

Sterling was trying to force himself to have a good time. It wasn't working for the most part. It was hard to smile and laugh when all he wanted was to be left alone. Being a good son, he spent a surprising amount of time enjoying Sierra's company. He had been right about her intelligence. She spoke proudly about her cofounding and running a private equity firm in New York.

Several times throughout the evening, he felt his mother's gaze trail after him. No doubt that she gloated, thinking that she'd found him the perfect woman. Who knows? Maybe she had. Maybe if he did settle down, everyone would get off his back. But was he the type who married for convenience?

For all of Sierra's obvious charm, she didn't hold a candle to the one who had stolen his heart eighteen months ago. A woman whose body heat he'd missed every night since.

"How about a refill?" Sterling asked, noticing Sierra's empty glass.

"That would be great. Thank you."

Sterling waltzed away and made his way over to the bar. While he waited for his drinks, his brothers flanked him.

"So how's it going?" Jonas asked.

"Don't speak to me," Sterling said with even annoyance. "You tricked me."

"I don't know what you're talking about," Jonas lied. "I think that it's an incredible stroke of luck that you and the lovely Sierra Edwards happen to hook up here. You seem to be really getting along."

"Did your wife send you over here to say that to me?" Sterling asked.

"Yep," Jonas admitted, unashamed. "I do what I'm told."

Quentin laughed.

"I'll get you back for this—both of you."

"Me?" Q chuckled. "I have nothing to do with this. And I say count yourself lucky that it's just a date and not an engagement."

"Really? I can hardly tell the difference."

"Trust me. You'd know the difference."

"Here you go, Mr. Hinton." The bartender handed him his drinks.

Sterling turned from the bar only to run into his father. "Sterling, my boy. Glad to see you could make it for your old man."

"Old man?" Sterling frowned. "I don't know about that. You still seem young as ever to me."

Roger laughed as he puffed on his cigar. "Well, you certainly seem like you're enjoying yourself this evening. Sierra seems like a nice young woman. Did you know that her father is the head of Simmon's Corp?"

Sterling glanced over at Quentin.

"Told you," he singsonged.

"The answer's no, Dad."

"What? I was just saying."

The brothers laughed and walked off, leaving Roger to shout the departing words. "Just think about it."

"Unbelievable." Sterling shook his head.

"Actually," Q said, scoping Sterling's date out from a distance. "I don't know what you're complaining about. At least they hooked you with a hot chick."

"You only think that because she has breasts."

"Big breasts," Quentin corrected with a laugh. "My marriage would've lasted at least three more months if Lizzie could fill a B-cup."

"You have issues," Jonas laughed.

"Big issues," Sterling agreed. He noticed Q constantly checking his watch and glancing around. "Who are you looking for?"

A broad and almost sly smile covered Q's face. "My date…if she decides to come."

"If?" Jonas and Sterling inquired, snickering.

"You mean some smart woman may have actually stood you up?" Sterling said. "First starting your own business and now this?"

Quentin didn't laugh at the joke. He sighed, his easy smile MIA. "It's a real possibility."

"Whoa. This sound serious." Jonas wrapped an arm around Q's shoulder. "Are you telling us what I think you're telling us?"

Miracle of miracles, Q blushed. "I'm afraid so. I really care for this girl." He glanced at Sterling. "I know *you* may never approve."

"Me?"

Quentin opened his mouth to explain, but then spotted the woman he'd been waiting for and broke out into a smile. "I don't believe it. She came."

Sterling turned his head, but his jaw dropped in surprise at seeing a smiling Alyssa stroll casually back into his life. What was worse was seeing a lovestruck Quentin rush up to her with open arms.

Chapter 28

Alyssa smiled as Quentin greeted her with a brief hug and a casual kiss against her cheek. As she glanced around, she took in the party's elaborate decorations and huge crowd and wondered for the umpteenth time whether she was about to make the biggest mistake in her life.

Probably.

"I can't tell you how happy I am you decided to come," Q said.

She smiled and clutched the glittering silver gift box—her excuse for attending this thing in the first place.

"I don't believe it," Roger boomed. "Is that little Ally?"

When Alyssa turned toward the birthday boy, Quentin's arm fell from her shoulders to loop around her waist. "Hello, Mr. Hinton."

"Aren't you a sight for sore eyes?" He approached and delivered his kiss against her cheek. "I haven't seen you since…"

Alyssa dropped her head. "Yes. It's been a while." Then belatedly she handed over her gift. "Happy birthday."

"Now you know that you didn't have to do this. It's good enough just to see you." His gaze swung low to his son's arm wrapped around her waist. He didn't comment, but instead seemed to sigh with acceptance.

Suddenly self-conscious, Alyssa pushed his arm down. It wasn't two seconds before it was back.

"Well you two enjoy yourselves. Kitty is around here somewhere. I'm sure she'll be thrilled to see you." He nodded toward Q with a look that said we'll-talk-later.

"Would you like something to drink?" Quentin asked, eagerly.

"Sure," she agreed and then relaxed when he rushed off.

"Ally. Is that you?"

Alyssa turned and saw a cotton-haired Beatrice sneaking over in a black-and-white serving uniform. "My goodness. You're still beautiful as ever."

Alyssa ran a hand down her long, white, beaded dress, which came with a matching beaded headband

and white feather. "Thanks. It wasn't easy finding a twenties costume on such short notice."

Clearly, not wanting to talk about fashion, the old maid leaned close and whispered, "So have you finally done it? Are you and Mister Quentin an item now?"

The assumption made Alyssa laugh. "No. We're just friends."

"Humph! That man ain't tryna be your friend." She glanced around and knew that she needed to get back to work. "We'll talk later."

Alyssa smiled and shook her head. She nervously scanned the crowd again and finally landed on the man that she really came to see.

Sterling.

The moment their eyes clashed, a fire ignited and scorched her from the inside out. The instant and painful attraction caused a fresh rush of tears to burn her eyes. He was the most beautiful sight to behold. He towered above the crowd. His stern and disapproving glare made him look more like a stone statue than a living, breathing man.

"Here's your drink," Q said, rushing back to her side.

"Thanks." She flashed him a smile then glanced back toward Sterling.

He was gone.

Alyssa's heart sank.

This was a mistake. The realization hit her so hard her knees buckled.

"Are you all right?" Q asked, his expression a mask of concern.

"Yeah." She nodded and took a long gulp of her drink.

Q chuckled. "Thirsty?"

"Something like that." She drained the rest of her glass and willed the alcohol to kick into her bloodstream faster.

"How about a dance?"

"No. I don't—"

"Come on. It'll be fun." Q took her empty glass and set it down on a passing tray then led her toward the floor. At first she took consolation in the fact that at least the music was upbeat, but the minute she and Quentin stepped on the dance floor, the big dance number was replaced by a slow song. Couples gathered close and literally danced cheek to cheek. If Alyssa didn't know better, she would swear that the sudden tempo shift was prearranged.

With no resistance, Alyssa allowed Quentin to pull her into his embrace. He took the lead and glided her around the floor with the fluid style of a modern Fred Astaire. Had it been another time...or a different brother, Alyssa was sure that she would have been swept away in the moment.

If only...

Alyssa closed her eyes and laid her head against Quentin's. "I don't think I can stay long," she said. She wanted to go home.

"What?" Q leaned his head back so that he could

look at her. He was clearly surprised to see tears shining in her eyes. "Whoa. What is it?"

She shook her head. "I'm sorry. But I shouldn't have come. I don't belong here."

"Of course you do." He gently wiped one of her stray tears from her face. "I invited you here because…well, I think you know why."

Alyssa continued to shake her head. Her tears started flowing faster. "Q, don't."

"Alice—"

"Don't." She closed her eyes in hopes of stemming the flow. "You don't understand."

He frowned as they rocked back and forth. "Make me understand."

The glass in Sterling's hand broke.

Sierra's and his mother's gasps drew his attention before the throbbing pain in his hand.

"My goodness. You're bleeding," Kitty announced and then glanced around. "Beatrice, get me something for Sterling's hand."

"Yes, ma'am."

Another employee quickly took the broken glass from his hand.

"Are you all right, darling?" his mother asked.

"Yeah, yeah." He blinked and then took the white napkin Beatrice offered. As he wrapped his hand, he joked, "Guess I don't know my own strength."

The small group fluttered awkward smiles.

"I better go into the house and clean this up." He

turned and stormed off. Against his will, his gaze shot back over to the dance floor. The sight of Alyssa locked in his brother's embrace had the effect of a jagged knife plunging into what was left of his heart. He tried to drag in a deep breath but the pain he felt exuded from his tear ducts causing his vision to blur.

"Hey, Sterling," Jonas called, approaching.

Sterling made a sharp right and marched to the main house.

Jonas called again; Sterling ignored his older brother. He had to get away before he either melted down or torched the place—and right now he was leaning toward the latter.

Avoiding the traffic on the bottom floor bathrooms, Sterling jogged upstairs and went to the bathroom adjoining his bedroom. It turned out that the cut on his hand wasn't as bad as it first appeared and he took his time to clean it up. One thing he was trying to do was avoid looking into the mirror. Again, his willpower was shot to hell and he stole a glance.

A broken man stared back.

Instead of answering Quentin's question, Alyssa pried his arms from around her waist and tried to ease away. "I'm sorry. This is not the place. Please understand." She turned, but Quentin grasped her hand.

"If you don't want to talk right here then let's go somewhere we can be alone," he suggested.

"Q—"

"Please," he added. "I don't want you to go."

The music's tempo shifted into another dance number. In order to be heard, Quentin led Alyssa off the dance floor and then continued to press his case. "Let's go into the house and we can talk there."

They glanced up at the house, but it was teeming with people.

"Well, what about the solarium. I know no one is there. We can sit down and talk."

Alyssa kept shaking her head.

"No funny stuff," he promised. "Something is obviously bothering you and as your friend I want to help."

At last she stopped shaking her head. She studied him, weighed his sincerity.

"We *are* friends, right?" he asked.

Finally, her lips twitched upward.

"All right. I'm going to get us a bottle of wine and some glasses. Why don't you meet me there?"

Doubt etched back into her features.

Q smiled reassuringly. "It'll give you a few minutes to dry your eyes."

She relented. "Okay."

Sterling flipped off the bathroom's light switch and then wondered whether he should return to the party. It would save him from having to watch Quentin and Alyssa flaunt their relationship in front of him.

Quentin and Alyssa.

The dagger plunged deeper into his chest as unbidden images of Alyssa flooded back into his head. Eighteen months of hard work went up in smoke.

Somberly, Sterling walked over to his bedroom window and stared down at the crowd. At that moment, everyone stopped what they were doing and started singing "Happy Birthday" to his proud and beaming father.

Sterling looked on without a smile. He couldn't. He felt like a dying man.

He told himself not to do it, but the temptation to seek Alyssa out in the crowd overwhelmed him. He almost sighed in relief when he didn't spot her. Then, his gaze snagged on a white dress, heading west from the party. Sterling frowned, and then quickly scanned the perimeter again until he saw his brother making a slow progression toward one of the bars.

The solarium.

The moment Alyssa strolled inside the solarium, she felt as if she had somehow transported back in time. It was another full moon and another night where she was waiting for Quentin. She wondered whether she really should tell him about the brief affair between her and Sterling. Should she tell him that even after all this time, she still loved him?

That she craved him?

A hand brushed against her shoulder. She whirled around and gasped, "Sterling." She stepped back.

"I take it you were waiting for someone else... *again.*"

The implication was clear. "What are you doing here?"

"I was about to ask you that same question."

Alyssa swallowed. Sterling's dominating presence absorbed most of the oxygen.

"Maybe I should just ask you how long you've been with Quentin?"

She frowned. "Quentin and I—"

"You know what? It doesn't matter." He stepped back, shaking his head. "*He* was who you really wanted anyway."

"Did you *forget* that you were the one who dumped me?"

"So you ran to my brother?" he accused. "You like to stay in the family, is that it?"

Her hand whipped across his face. Hard.

"How fast did you go to him?"

She slapped him again. Harder.

"Is he a better lover?"

Slap!

Sterling grabbed her hand and pushed her back up against a stone ledge. He could no longer hide his hurt and anger behind a carefully constructed mask. "Answer the question," he hissed. "Does he make you feel the way I do?"

Alyssa's mind went blank at the feel of Sterling's steel erection pressed against her pelvis while his free hand pulled up her dress. "When he touches you, does it make you hot?"

She couldn't breathe.

"Do you purr his name when he hits your spot, hmm? Do you like to compare us? Is that it?"

"Sterling…"

"What is it, baby?" He thrust his hand into her panties and slid his finger inside her. "Look at how wet you are," he groaned against her ear. "I bet you don't get this wet for him, do you? Hmm?" Sterling dropped his head down and dragged his lips against the long column of her neck.

"Sterling…"

"Open your legs wider for me, baby," he ordered. "Let me feel you."

She obeyed and her knees nearly buckled when he slipped in a second finger. "Oh, yeah," he panted. "This belongs to me, doesn't it, baby? *You* belong to me. Don't you?" He released her hand and pulled up the other side of her dress. "Do you know how much I missed you, baby? Do you know how hard I've tried to forget what it feels like to be buried deep inside you?"

Heady from his confession, Alyssa's hands fumbled with his zipper. Her body had gone haywire and she sought the one thing that it desperately needed. Within seconds, she freed his unbending erection and he pushed her panties aside and penetrated her with one mighty thrust. At that thrilling moment, there was an undeniable click in her head—the coming together of two puzzle pieces snapping in place.

"You belong to me," he insisted as his hips pumped and then rotated. "Say it," he ordered. "You'll always belong to me."

"Yes, God, yes." Alyssa's head fell back as her

arms wrapped around his thick neck to anchor her in place. Their lips sought and found each other's as he lifted her and held her at an angle where his thick shaft rubbed against her throbbing clit.

Their body heat escalated while his thrusts shortened but deepened. He couldn't get enough of her. He never wanted to get enough.

He'd been a fool to have let her go.

A fool to throw away happiness.

A fool even now if she would or could ever forgive him.

"I love you, Alyssa," he groaned, burying his face into the crook of her neck. "I'm never going to let you go again. You hear me? Never."

The raw emotion in his voice touched and swelled her heart. It was the first time she'd heard the words from him and everything, from the way he touched her to the way he said her name. The only thing she didn't understand was why. Why had he pushed her away? Why had he been so willing to throw away her heart?

As Sterling continued to rock her body those questions melted away in her mind. All she could do was revel in this glorious moment. When it was over, he could just as easily push her away and break her heart again.

And it was worth the risk.

To be with him in whatever way would always be worth the risk.

Alyssa's sighs and moans went up and down a

musical scale. Raw pleasure enfolded them into its arms while the music from the party played on. Alyssa's hands fell to Sterling's shoulders, her fingers dug into his corded muscles as her body quivered and then exploded.

Sterling's release roared through him with all the force of a hurricane. He trembled as he spilled everything he had into this woman.

His fear.

His heart.

His love.

For long seconds afterward, they remained connected and panting for breath. Neither knew what had just happened or why.

But they didn't regret it.

When the silence stretched too long, it begged for truth.

"I'm not dating him," she whispered. "I've never slept with him. We're just friends."

Sterling closed his eyes as relief flooded every fiber of his being. At last, he pulled out, adjusted his clothes. Once done, he looked down into her moonlit face. Where should he begin? "I—"

"Why?" she asked. Her eyes filled with tears. "Just tell me why. I deserve that much, don't I?"

Sterling's eyes glossed, his tears held back by the thinnest thread of willpower. "Guilt," he admitted. He watched as her expression collapsed in confusion. "I—I've known you since…" He shook his head. "I feel like, even now, that I've crossed a line. A part of me believes strongly that I've taken advantage of you—that I have broken some forbidden rule. I was good friends with your father for God's sakes. He even left me a letter…." His voice shook.

"What letter?"

He drew a deep breath and explained himself. "The day you returned to L.A., I received a letter from your father's attorney. He asked me to look out for you…because he trusted me to not take advantage of you." His shoulders dropped low. "He was wrong to do that."

"What? No." She moved closer to him and cupped his face in her hands. "If anything, my father would have been thrilled. He loved and respected you. You're a man of character and conviction—the kind of man he'd *want* me to fall in love with." She paused and blinked away tears. "The kind of man I *did* fall in love with. The man I still love."

Sterling searched her face, wondering how what she said could be true. "How? After what I…"

"Because you've always been there. Even these past eighteen months, you've never left my heart. I wish you would have come to me about this—this guilt. I would've reassured you that the only thing that matters is how we feel about each other. That's it. It's not other people. It's not our ages. It's just us."

A slow smile eased across Sterling's face. "I don't deserve you."

"Of course not." She smiled. "And I don't deserve you."

Sterling pulled her against him and then kissed her with a heart fully healed.

Suddenly, Alyssa drew back with a gasp. "Oh my God. I forgot!"

Sterling frowned.

"Quentin," she stressed. "He was supposed to be coming out here."

Sterling jerked his head back and looked over his shoulder. All he saw was his mother's plants and rare orchids.

"He should have been here by now," she whispered. "What if he saw us?"

"I thought you said that you were just friends?"

"We are…but I know Q wants to be more," she admitted.

Sterling knew that, as well, which meant that the discovery was worse for him than her. How on earth would he be able to explain this? No way would his brother see this for anything other than the betrayal that it was. "Stay here," he said. He moved back toward the front door of the solarium and then stopped when he saw a bottle of champagne and two glasses on the floor.

Quentin had seen them.

Chapter 29

"Quentin!" Sterling shouted as he raced out of the solarium. He had no idea what he was going to say to his brother if or once he caught up with him. He had been so blinded by jealousy he hadn't thought his actions through. Now that he'd been caught making love to his brother's date, he feared that he may have just damaged his relationship with his brother beyond repair.

"Sterling, wait!" Alyssa shouted, taking off behind him.

Sterling rounded a bend and trekked past a great oak before he spotted Quentin. "Q, hold up!"

His brother shot him the bird but kept marching back toward their father's birthday party. The band had the crowd in full sway as Quentin plowed through in his fierce determination to put as much distance between him and Sterling as possible.

Sterling couldn't let sleeping dogs lie. His long athletic legs carried him across the lawn and through the parting crowd in record time. Yet, when he laid a hand upon his brother's shoulder, he was caught off guard by Quentin's own amazing speed when he whipped around and landed a punch that reeled Sterling back a few steps.

A loud gasp went up and then every neck and eye swiveled.

"You stay the hell away from me," Quentin growled. "As far as I'm concerned we're not friends and we're not brothers."

Alyssa caught up to the two brothers. Sterling being her immediate concern, she took his side. "You're bleeding."

Quentin hardened his jaw as his eyes glazed over. "So how long?"

"What the hell is going on over here?" Roger snapped, shouldering his way through the crowd. "Quentin, have you been drinking?"

Q laughed. "Not yet."

Sterling glanced around the crowd, his discomfort evident on his face. "Q, let's just go into the house so we can talk."

Quentin didn't even look tempted by the offer. His gaze swung between Sterling and Alyssa, and then he held up his hands and backed away. "I've said all I'm going to say. You just stay the hell away from me. Both of you."

Jonas stepped into the ring made by the crowd but his refereeing skills weren't needed, as Quentin turned on his heels and took off.

Once gone, everyone's attention returned to Sterling and Alyssa.

"All right, everyone. Show's over," Roger announced. "More champagne."

The crowd tittered but slowly they broke up into smaller clusters.

"Are you okay?" Alyssa asked, hugging his waist.

Sterling didn't hear the question. "He's never going to forgive me."

"Sure he will. He just needs time to calm down."

Sterling shook his head. No one held a grudge like Quentin—except maybe their father.

"I need to see you two in my office," Roger hissed and then marched toward the house as if there wouldn't be a voice of dissension.

He was right.

Arm in arm, Sterling and Alyssa followed Roger as if they were headed toward the gallows. When Alyssa caught a few sympathetic looks from Beatrice, Jamie and Lidi, she tried her best to give them a reassuring smile.

But she wasn't fooling anyone.

For the first time in her life, she was about to experience Roger Hinton's famous "behind-the-office-door" temper tantrums.

"Somebody wanna tell me what the hell is going on around here?" Roger snapped before Alyssa's bottom hit the chair. "Sterling, I thought you were here with Barbara Anne's daughter?"

"Yes, sir, but—"

"And weren't you with Quentin earlier?" he asked Alyssa.

"Yes, sir, but—"

"So what is this, some kind of date swapping going on?" Roger thundered. "And what are you doing with Alfred's daughter down at the solarium?"

"Dad, I can explain—"

"You know what? Don't answer that. You're consenting adults and I'm too old to try and keep up with you young people and your drama." He drew in a deep breath and eyed both Sterling and Alyssa. He noticed how their hands remained interlocked. "However, Kitty would kill me if I didn't find out if you two were serious." He cleared his throat. "Are you?"

Despite the throb of his busted bottom lip, Sterling smiled down at the love of his life. "Yes, Dad." He pulled Alyssa up from her chair and pressed her body against his. "Tell Mom that it's very serious *and* that she may want to get hold of that wedding planner *very* soon."

"Well then." Roger lit up. "That's good news. I— I mean other than that unfortunate business with Quentin punching you in the face. Good news indeed." He headed back toward the party as if he couldn't wait to share this latest news with his wife.

However, when he opened his office door, his staff: Beatrice, Jamie, Lidi, James and Antonio toppled over and spilled into the office.

Alyssa smacked a hand over her mouth, but it failed to contain her laughter.

"What on earth?" He frowned at the group.

Everyone scrambled back onto their feet, but instead of being ashamed for having been caught snooping, they all raced to snatch Alyssa from Sterling's arm for hugs and to share in the couple's excitement. It had taken time, but Alyssa was finally marrying a Hinton.

Back at the Dollhouse...

Chapter 30

Now...

"So you walked in on them?" Xavier concluded.

"Lucky me, huh?" Quentin shared a sloppy smile. He was way past being drunk and honestly didn't care. "I mean there I was catching my *big* brother..." He sniffed and waved the memory off. "Whatever. It doesn't matter. I don't care what they do anymore. They are both dead to me now."

Xavier stared at Quentin and saw the lie for what it was. After hearing this story, he couldn't help but be intrigued by this woman who'd snared the hearts of two brothers and unwittingly driven a wedge between them.

"You haven't talked to your brother since?"

"Don't see the point. He and Alyssa had tried to explain the situation all over my answering machine…but I've never returned their call."

Xavier shook his head. "He's your brother."

"Yeah. The same brother who tried to make me ashamed of my attraction to his now fiancée."

"They're engaged?"

"Yep." He stared at the empty bottle on the table. "Wedding is next week," he sang.

"And you're not going?" his cousin asked incredulously.

"What? And stand there like an idiot when he gives her our last name?"

Xavier laughed and shook his head. "Look, we're best friends and all but I have to tell you this. You're being incredibly selfish right now. We've been best friends for over twenty years and I have seen your brothers stick by you and support you through every decision you've made. And most of them have been pretty bad."

"Thanks a lot."

"You're welcome." He studied his friend again. "Look, we're probably best friends because we're a lot alike. I don't know that much about falling in love or any of that soul mate stuff people rave about, but I do know that when people find it they…they change. First they love it, then they fight it and push it away and then if they're lucky it comes back to them. Sounds like your brother is damn lucky it came back to him, if you ask me. Believe it or not, it's not always about *you,* man."

Quentin shifted uncomfortably.

"You want to know what I think?" Xavier asked.

"I'm not so sure."

"I think if anything ever did happen between you and this Alyssa that it would have ended the same way that all your relationships end. You get bored and then move on to the next woman. You're not like your brothers Jonas and Sterling. Monogamy isn't in your DNA."

Quentin's expression twisted sourly. "C'mon, man. You're supposed to be on my side, remember?"

"I am on your side. I also happen to remember when you thought Ashlee Dunham was the love of your life back in college. Then there was that time that you fell in love with Sasha something or another. I think she was an airline stewardess. Then there was Rachel—"

"All right. All right. I get it."

"Face it," Xavier pressed. "No matter how this went down, you need to let it go and for once in your life, be there for your brother. You owe him at least that much."

Epilogue

Alyssa had always dreamed of her wedding day. The journey from being that little girl to the woman she was now, in some ways seemed long and in others so very short. As she looked at her reflection in the full-length mirror, her gaze roamed over every detail in her white wedding dress and she could feel another wave of tears threaten to ruin her makeup.

"I wish your father was here to see you," Estelle said, looking on. "He would have been so proud."

"Ooh. You look pretty," Jessica said, staring up at her.

"Thank you, sweetheart." She beamed down at her little sister, pleased to see her father so clearly in her face.

"I'm supposed to give you this." Jessica handed her a folded slip of paper. "It's from Sterling."

She frowned with a brief fear that her fiancé had changed his mind and was about to leave her standing at the altar. But instead, the brief message warmed her soul.

Twenty minutes before I make you my wife.
Can't wait.
S.

"It must be good news." Estelle said, winking.

"The best. I'm about to marry the love of my life."

"Hallelujah." Tangela snickered as she finished buttoning the tiny buttons on the back of Alyssa's dress. "But I guess love takes time."

Alyssa agreed. She just wished that Quentin would be there. It was the one blight on this otherwise perfect day. Somehow both she and Sterling had managed to hurt him in ways they feared that Quentin could never forgive. Turned out, she'd become the very heartbreaker he'd predicted she would be.

Finally, it was time.

The second the wedding march began, Alyssa stepped out onto the Hintons' lush green lawn and tried to control her pounding heart. It was a beautiful spring evening. Her heart swelled at the sight of so many family and friends gathered there on her special day. Beatrice, James, Antonio, Jamie and Lidi—all sat up front waving and crying.

The smile stretched across Sterling's face as she moved toward him and their future warmed her to her core. The look in his eyes radiated with love and she basked in all its glory.

Her gaze fluttered to his right. There, standing with his hands crossed before him, was Jonas…and Quentin. His expression was unreadable…and if she wasn't mistaken one side of his face looked twice its usual size. But at least he came. For now, that was enough. The tears she had barely held in check finally flowed freely down her face as she took her place next to Sterling and faced the preacher.

When they were finally pronounced man and wife, Alyssa slid into her husband's arms, pleased with the knowledge that her life was a hell of a lot better than any childhood fantasy.

A love that's out of this world...

Cosmic Rendezvous

Favorite author
Robyn Amos

For aerospace engineer Shelly London, a top-secret
space project could be her big break—until she butts
heads with sexy hotshot astronaut Lincoln Ripley, who
launches her hormones right into orbit. Lincoln's got
a double mission: catch a saboteur...then take off with
Shelly for a rendezvous with love.

"Lilah's List is...a fun story that
holds one's interest from page one."
—*Romantic Times BOOKreviews*

**Coming the first week of April 2009
wherever books are sold.**

KIMANI™
ROMANCE

*The "Triple Threat" Donovan brothers are back...
and last-man-standing Trent is about to roll the
dice on falling in love.*

Defying
DESIRE

Book #3 in *The Donovan Brothers*

A.C. Arthur

When it comes to men, model Tia St. Claire wants no
strings, just flings. But navy SEAL Trent Donovan stirs
defiant longings she can't deny. Happily unattached,
Trent has dedicated his career to duty and danger, until
desire—and Tia—changes everything.

*Coming the first week of April 2009
wherever books are sold.*

KIMANI™
ROMANCE

www.kimanipress.com
www.myspace.com/kimanipress

KPACA1090409

He's an irresistible recipe—for trouble!

Sugar RUSH

elaine overton

Life is sweet for bakery owner Sophie Mayfield.
She's saved her family business from a takeover, and
hired talented baker Eliot Wright to help sales. Eliot
is as appealing—and oh-so-chocolate-fine—as he is
hardworking. But when Sophie discovers Eliot is not
what he seems, Eliot must regain Sophie's trust—and
prove he's her permanent sweet spot.

_Coming the first week of April 2009
wherever books are sold._

KIMANI™
ROMANCE

www.kimanipress.com
www.myspace.com/kimanipress

KPEO1110409

REQUEST YOUR FREE BOOKS!

2 FREE NOVELS
PLUS 2 FREE GIFTS!

KIMANI™ ROMANCE

Love's ultimate destination!

YES! Please send me 2 FREE Kimani™ Romance novels and my 2 FREE gifts (gifts are worth about $10). After receiving them, if I don't wish to receive any more books, I can return the shipping statement marked "cancel." If I don't cancel, I will receive 4 brand-new novels every month and be billed just $4.69 per book in the U.S. or $5.24 per book in Canada, plus 25¢ shipping and handling per book and applicable taxes, if any*. That's a savings of over 20% off the cover price! I understand that accepting the 2 free books and gifts places me under no obligation to buy anything. I can always return a shipment and cancel at any time. Even if I never buy another book from Kimani Press, the two free books and gifts are mine to keep forever.

168 XDN EF2D   368 XDN EF3T

Name	(PLEASE PRINT)	
Address		Apt. #
City	State/Prov.	Zip/Postal Code

Signature (if under 18, a parent or guardian must sign)

Mail to **The Reader Service:**
IN U.S.A.: P.O. Box 1867, Buffalo, NY 14240-1867
IN CANADA: P.O. Box 609, Fort Erie, Ontario L2A 5X3

Not valid to current subscribers of Kimani Romance books.

Want to try two free books from another line?
Call 1-800-873-8635 or visit www.morefreebooks.com.

* Terms and prices subject to change without notice. N.Y. residents add applicable sales tax. Canadian residents will be charged applicable provincial taxes and GST. Offer not valid in Quebec. This offer is limited to one order per household. All orders subject to approval. Credit or debit balances in a customer's account(s) may be offset by any other outstanding balance owed by or to the customer. Please allow 4 to 6 weeks for delivery. Offer available while quantities last.

Your Privacy: Kimani Press is committed to protecting your privacy. Our Privacy Policy is available online at www.eHarlequin.com or upon request from the Reader Service. From time to time we make our lists of customers available to reputable third parties who may have a product or service of interest to you. If you would prefer we not share your name and address, please check here. ☐

KROM08R

National bestselling author

ROCHELLE ALERS

Naughty

Parties, paparazzi, red-carpet catfights…

Wild child Breanna Parker's antics have
always been a ploy to gain attention from
her diva mother and record-producer father.
As her marriage implodes, Bree moves to
Rome. There she meets charismatic Reuben,
who becomes both her romantic and business
partner. But just as she's enjoying her
successful new life, Bree is confronted
with a devastating scandal that threatens
everything she's worked so hard for.…

Coming the first week of March 2009
wherever books are sold.

KIMANI PRESS™

www.kimanipress.com
www.myspace.com/kimanipress

KPRA1280309

What if you met your future soul mate, but were too busy to give them the time of day?

ANGELA BASSETT & COURTNEY B. VANCE

THE *NEW YORK TIMES* BESTSELLING REAL-LIFE STORY...

friends: a love story

They ran for years as friends in the same circles, had some hits—but mostly misses—with other partners and shared one dreadful first date together. Then, Courtney and Angela connected.

Experience the real-life love story of this inspirational African-American celebrity couple. See how they've carved a meaningful life together despite humble beginnings, family tragedy and the ups and downs of stardom with love, faith and determination.

**Available the first week of February 2009
wherever books are sold.**

KIMANI PRESS™

**www.kimanipress.com
www.myspace.com/kimanipress** KPABCBV1210209